Subway Girl

Donna Beck

For Jack and Austin,

the loves of my life.

ACKNOWLEDGMENTS

Thank you "Lovely Bob" from Chicago for taking an interest in this story and becoming my benevolent editor. Your encouragement has been as valuable as your sharp eye, and I am truly grateful to know you.

CONTENTS

1 - STRAY DOGS

People always say your life can change in an instant, but I thought they meant something drastic had to happen, like a car accident, or maybe a blood vessel burst in your brain. Or it could be that something really lucky happens, such as being spotted by a talent agent, or winning the lottery. I didn't know that your life could change in an instant but that it would not instantly change. What I mean is, something could happen, something subtle, and you may not realize it at the time but it changes the course of your life. You could be going along in a rut, not even knowing how deep the rut is and how unlikely it is that you will ever get out of it, when something happens that lifts you out of the rut and your life takes a slightly different trajectory. Months later you look back and think how stunning, how utterly remarkable it is that your life ever changed at all. That is what happened to me last summer, and it started when a complete stranger hugged me.

That may sound kind of corny or even churchy, but you would have to understand what kind of a guy I was back then, what kind of a person I had become and how I was living. I was hanging out with this guy Robbie who was a homeless panhandler. I wasn't either of those things, but people often mistook me for a homeless person. I was getting the weathered look of a guy who lives outdoors. The truth is I wasn't technically homeless, but I didn't go home for days at a time.

My hair was in dreadlocks, which contributed to the homeless impression. Not the cool kind of dreadlocks that a guy in a band might have, mine were nasty. I didn't even set out to have dreadlocks, it just happened when I wore a knit cap for a month and neglected to comb my somewhat coarse hair. It got a few matted spots in the back and I didn't bother to do anything about it. By the time the weather warmed up and I took my cap off, I had a dreadful hairdo. Not neat and symmetrical dreadlocks. I had a few big ones in the back, a few small ones all around, and some hair that just didn't conform. To my surprise, my dreads did not cause people to stare at me. In fact, it had the opposite effect. People avoided me and gave me space. I looked homeless which made people assume I must be crazy or a drug addict and they left me alone. I kind of liked the feeling of being invisible. I realized if you wear headphones, sunglasses, and a cap, you can go days on end without anyone talking to you or trying to mess with you.

One particular day, I was standing next to Robbie, who was asking people getting off the subway for a dollar. It works better to ask for a specific amount rather than just ask for change. I was standing about five feet away from him so that he would look alone, which is also better for panhandling, but we could still converse and joke around with each other. Robbie and I liked to try and make each other laugh while we were acting like we didn't know each other. I was usually a pretty shy person, but when people look right through you it gets easy to be bold sometimes. Most people wouldn't look my way, so I felt comfortable saying crazy things to strangers. This time I was pretending like random women getting off the subway were my girlfriend coming home from work all happy to see me. I would hold my arms open and pucker my lips. This got a good laugh out of Robbie, so I started to say to a few of them "Hey honey, I missed you. Where's my kiss?"

Of course they ignored me and kept walking, but then suddenly one stopped. She stopped and looked at my face, which kind of startled me since most people don't do that. She stopped and said, "I won't kiss you, but I will give you a hug." I thought she was joking, but when she took a few steps towards me, I figured she was some sort of religious zealot. I got ready for a "churchy" hug expecting her to put her arms on my shoulders and give me a few pats and tell me that Jesus loves me. But that is not what happened.

She set her briefcase down on the ground and put her arms around me and hugged me like she knew me, like she was completely comfortable. It wasn't just an upper body hug. She sort of folded herself into me and I could feel her legs touching mine. And she held on for a long time. In actuality, it was probably five seconds, but I wasn't expecting her to do that. I could hear Robbie laughing and practically screaming, hooting and hollering, but I stayed quiet and still, not wanting to ruin the moment.

She released her hug and I mumbled, "Thank you." She looked me right in the eyes and said, "You're welcome," then picked up her briefcase, turned, and walked away.

I was so startled I started shaking. "Go after her, man! There's your chance. She wants you, man!" Robbie laughed, doubling over and slapping his knees. "I can't believe it, man. Go after her!" But I could not explain to Robbie that I didn't want to spoil it. I did not want to scare her or follow her. I wanted to go think about what had just happened, so I walked in the direction she went without looking for her, just trying to get away from Robbie. Back to the bustling world where I was invisible so I could sit down and think. I sat down next to a wall and thought about every detail that had just happened so I wouldn't forget it.

She was wearing a business suit, a grey skirt and matching jacket, but her shirt was hot pink and shiny, like the kind you could wear out at night. Her clothes and briefcase made her seem mature, but I could see in her face that she had to be in her twenties. She smelled really good. She had blond hair that was pinned up. She was a lot shorter than me. She was good at hugging. Her eyes were blue. I didn't want to forget anything, but then I started to question if it really happened, it seemed so bizarre. But I'm not crazy and I don't do drugs. A pretty girl thought I was huggable, and I thought she was very brave.

The next day I returned to the exact same spot at the exact same time hoping to see her again, just to make sure she was real. I was glad Robbie wasn't around. I thought about how my mom used to tell us not to feed stray dogs or they will never go away. I felt like a stray dog.

I tried to get a good look at every blond that got off the subway. Then I saw her. It seemed like she might be looking for me too. She had her head up when she got off the subway and I saw a quick grin before she looked down and kept her eyes on the ground as she walked. I expected she would walk right past me, which would be okay. I was just so relieved to see her again, to validate that it was real. I did not expect her to acknowledge me.

But she walked straight up to me and said "Where's my hug?" She actually said that like it was the most natural thing in the world, so of course I hugged her. And it was amazing, I heard her sigh, or I felt it. It seemed like she relaxed in my arms, like she knew me and wasn't scared. Again, I held very still, trying not to ruin it by seeming to cop a feel or anything weird like that. I would have stayed in that position for days, but she released the hug and looked me straight in the face and said "Thank you." She actually thanked me, so I muttered a quick "You're welcome," and she picked up her briefcase and walked away.

I started shaking again, but not as bad this time. I was able to watch her walk for several yards so I could study her and remember everything about her. Her hair was blond and silky and fell past her shoulders. Today she had on black slacks and a royal blue cardigan with a white shirt underneath. She carried a black briefcase. Her shoes had small heels. She walked really fast.

Of course I went back the next day. This time I expected to see her and even planned my day around it. I went by my apartment that afternoon to brush my teeth and pick up some clean clothes. The reason I never go home is that I live in a tiny one-room apartment with two drug addicts. They were not always that bad, but things had gotten crazy and I never knew what would be going on there. I seldom went home, but I could not afford to move, so I continued to pay rent on a place I couldn't even feel comfortable in, but I could not give up the apartment. If I didn't have an address, I really would be homeless. Plus, I could afford 1/3 of the rent with my unemployment check and my check got mailed there. When that stopped, something would have to change, but I tried not to think about that.

I always knocked on the door of the apartment even though I have a key. I wanted them to know I was coming in so they could at least put the pipe away or turn the porn off or something. Even though I knocked and waited ten seconds to turn the key, Jeff looked startled. He was standing in the middle of the room naked. He mumbled "Hey" and headed towards the bathroom, the only place where there was any privacy.

"Wait!" I shouted. I knew if he went in there it might be hours before he came out. "Let me get my toothbrush first!" But he quickly shut and locked the door.

"Hey, man, I need my toothbrush." No answer. "Jeff! Just

give me my toothbrush! I need to take off."

He cracked open the door and tossed out a red toothbrush.

"That's not mine."

"That's the only one in here. Just rinse it with hot water."

I went downstairs to get my clothes. I stopped keeping clothes in the apartment because my roommates used to steal them. I never saw them wearing any of my clothes, but they all disappeared. I found a solution to the clothing dilemma when I saw a sign on the cork board in the entryway advertising for light housecleaning and laundry. There was a woman name Louisa downstairs and she would wash my clothes for 25 cents each. I would give her pants, a shirt, underwear and socks for a dollar. (She counted a pair of socks as one item, bless her soul.) But the best part was it gave me a safe place to keep clothes. I gave her a dollar and she handed me a clean set and I headed upstairs to change.

This time I just used the key since I knew Jeff was locked in the bathroom and would stay there, but instead I saw Thomas doing lines on the kitchen counter. I didn't even know where he came from: he didn't pass me in the hallway, but there he was. He actually yelled at me, "Hey, don't you knock?"

"I live here," I stated.

"Well I wasn't expecting you," he barked.

I didn't answer since Thomas was a hothead when he got high. I just wanted to change my clothes and get out of there, but there was no privacy so I just turned my back to get changed as quickly as possible. I dropped off my dirty clothes to Louisa and headed out. I walked to the dollar store and bought a toothbrush, a travel sized toothpaste, and a deodorant, which smelled all wrong, and that left me with only one dollar to eat that day. I used to try to keep myself on a five-dollar-a-day budget, which was really hard to do when I had as much as $150 in my pocket the day after my unemployment check came and I paid rent. My routine was to shove my money through a hole in my left pocket; that meant my cash would be safely stored in the lining of my jacket. I would keep just $5 in my right pocket, my cash for the day. I took a bird bath in the sink at a bathroom in a convenience store, but I had to buy something to get the "customers only" bathroom key, so I bought a granola bar and I still felt hungry. This was okay because I knew some restaurants that throw away perfectly good food every night. I just had to wait.

My upper pocket held my phone, charger, earphones and ID. My phone was my prized possession and that's how I treated it. My Dad still had me on his plan as long as I agreed to check in once a week, so I didn't have to pay for the phone bill, but I did have to find places to charge it. I didn't charge it in the apartment when my roommates were there – for obvious reasons.

The next day at the subway station, I stood in the same spot waiting for her. I scope out every blond woman that gets off the subway, but I don't see her. The subway moves on and the crowd thins out. I try not to feel disappointed, but I do. I wonder if she missed her subway and I decide to wait for the next one.

Again I search the crowd looking at the face of every blond, but I don't see her. I wondered if she purposely got off at the previous stop or the next one, to avoid me. Maybe she came to her senses and knew not to pet a stray dog.

I walked around a lot that night and stopped for a few naps. There are a few 24-hour places where I could hang out for an hour, such as a donut shop as long as I bought something, so I dipped into tomorrow's money for seventy cents. I can sleep sitting up with a cap pulled low and as long as I don't stay too long, I can get away with it. During the day I hang out at the library a lot. I may look scruffy sometimes, but I am young and I don't stink and I don't babble, so with a book in front of me I can really catch some z's. I even have a library card and sometimes I'll check out a paperback I can fit in my pocket and carry around. I've heard it said that NYC is such a literate city that even the homeless read. It seems to be true since I've seen other guys that are truly homeless with books. Again, I think it is a good shield to hide behind when avoiding the human race in a crowded city.

I think about the subway girl a lot that day and wonder what happened to her. I contemplate going back, but I don't want to be disappointed again so it is easier to act like I don't care, and I catch myself trying to make up mean things about her. But in the end either my curiosity, my boredom, or my loneliness wins out and I head back to the same spot at five o'clock. I really don't have anywhere else to be anyway.

This time I see her and I am sure she is looking for me. She walks right up to me and I said, "I missed you yesterday." I didn't plan to say it, it just came out and I immediately regretted it. "I was sick," she said. And then she hugged me. Didn't ask, just did it, not that I would have denied her or anything.

"Are you feeling better?" I asked while she was in my arms.

"I am. Thank you," she said. Then she released me and turned and walked away.

I watched her go and noted that she seemed sad today. Her voice was different. She wasn't walking as fast. She had on grey slacks and a black sweater. I wanted to follow her and talk to her, but again I was afraid I'd break the spell.

The next day was Saturday, but I knew I'd be back on Monday.

Saturday was my favorite day of the week, the only day that was different from the other six. On Saturdays I play soccer in the park, and it is the one time I forgot about how my daily life had become, and I felt like my old self, the young and optimistic Ray who moved to NYC with his buddy Carlos, back when we both had jobs.

Carlos and I had been buddies in high school and it was his idea to move to the city. He had a cousin who was the maintenance manager of a big office building and he said he could get us jobs. We were basically janitors, but we also go to fix stuff, which was cool. We had a room with some tools and parts where we worked, mostly on office chairs. I was amazed at how often people complained about a broken chair. We had tons of damaged chairs and we would scrap parts and repair chairs, then take out trash, clean and stock restrooms, change fluorescent lights, fill up the water bottles, stuff like that. It was a great job. At first we were always busy and could not believe we were so lucky to work in this nice office when the weather was freezing cold or scorching hot outside.

We got the apartment I still have – the one tiny room with a kitchen "area," which was really just a few cabinets and sink and tiny appliances along one wall. The only separate space was the tiny bathroom, the private domain of my current roommates. With Carlos it seemed small but bearable, since we didn't hate each other. Even though we worked together, lived together, and played on the same soccer team, we managed to get along.

Carlos and I had always played soccer and within weeks of

living here we managed to get in with a group that played every Saturday morning. We did not have organized practice, just showed up and played, although Carlos and I practiced together during the week. Carlos moved back home when we lost our jobs, but I stayed and continued to show up no matter how weird the rest of my life got. Moving home would make me feel like a failure. The only thing left for me at home since my mom died was my dad and brother, and they both resented me for not joining the family plumbing business. "You too good for us, Ray?" my brother would ask, and my dad would chime in with, "Ah, we don't need him." I knew my dad did not have enough business to pay both of his sons, so he seemed relieved when I found a job in the city.

I picked up my clean soccer uniform early every Saturday morning from Louisa and returned it to her stinky and sweaty every Saturday night. Louisa always said "Play hard" when she handed me my uniform. It seemed a really strange thing for her to say, but on weekdays she always told me "Work hard." I took her advice only on Saturdays.

I got to the park that Saturday, saw the guys kicking the ball around, and went up and said hello to Marcus, an older guy I've become friends with. He has a pretty wife and two little kids who come with him to the park sometimes. His wife always gives me a Gatorade. None of the guys know that I roam the city all week. They think I am normal and they treat me like normal, but we don't talk about anything besides soccer. Today Marcus asked me how Carlos was doing, but I have not talked to him so I just said "Fine."

After the game I went by the apartment and for some lucky reason, no one was there. I jumped at the chance to take a shower. There was no soap and the bottom of the bathtub was filthy and grimy, but it felt great to let the warm water run over my body. Really great. I kept thinking about "Subway Girl" and how nice she felt in my arms, how good it felt to touch somebody. In fact, I was thinking about it so much that I started to get hard and took advantage of this rare moment of privacy. Just in time too, as I heard a loud crash out in the main room. I didn't have a towel to dry off with, so I stood there shivering a while and listened to my two roommates yelling at each other in the other room. I used the outside of my jacket to dry myself off, got dressed, and got the hell out of there. They didn't even acknowledge me when I walked out. They were quiet and hovering over something on the coffee table I couldn't see, so I just headed to the door and reminded them "Five days 'til rent is due."

Sundays were sometimes easy, sometimes hard for me, because the library and a lot of businesses were closed, but churches were open and I knew a few that I could go to where people dressed casual and I wouldn't stand out if I just sat in the back. I had three different Catholic churches I could go to and this day I scored as one of them had a potluck in the parish hall after church. I was able to save the $4.30 I had left over for that day, which was good because something usually came up. The afternoon wasn't cold so I sat outside in the park. I even saw a soccer buddy who was practicing and got to kick the ball around for a bit. Then came the weekly Sunday afternoon call home where I told my dad I was looking for a job and asked how he was doing. He always asked when I was coming for a visit, but the price of a bus ticket was way out of my reach. I couldn't tell my dad I didn't have enough for a bus ticket, so instead I acted like I was busy on the weekends with soccer and friends and stuff. I don't know if he believed me or if he just wanted to believe me, but he didn't push it; the phone calls seemed enough to prove I wasn't dead or on drugs or anything.

Monday I went back to the subway station at 4:45 to wait for Subway Girl. Robbie was there this time and kept trying to talk to me and I was really nervous about it, so finally I just asked him,

"Hey, Robbie, if that pretty blonde girl hugs me today, can you do me a favor and just keep your mouth shut? I'll give you a buck to just stay quiet."

"Five bucks," Robbie answered.

"Hell no, two."

"Four."

"Dude, that's harsh. I'll pay you two."

"I'm gonna make a scene when your chick gets here."

"And I am gonna kick your ass."

"I'm gonna steal your four dollars and take your girl on a date to McDonald's. Let her order offa' the value menu." Robbie was laughing now, so I knew we had a deal.

Then I saw her. She was wearing a blue dress with boots today and she looked beautiful. My heart started racing. She smiled when she saw me and looked down as she walked straight to where I was standing. When she got to me she set her briefcase down and she hugged me, arms around my shoulders and mine around her waist. As soon as I could feel her loosening her grip, I let go and I really wanted to say something, but I didn't know what. She reached in the pocket of her dress and handed me a folded up piece of paper and said "Bye. See you tomorrow," and she turned and walked away.

"Four dollars, dude. Hope it was worth it."

I turned to Robbie and pulled the $2.00 out of my pocket and didn't answer. I wanted to get somewhere private and see what was on this piece of paper.

"Hell yeah, man, tomorrow I'm only chargin' ya $3.00!"

Robbie was laughing as I walked away. I found a place to sit by the wall and slowly unfolded the sheet of notebook paper. It was handwritten in black ink and said "My name is Alicia, and hugging you is the bright spot in my day."

I reread the note several times, said the name "Alicia" out loud, then folded the note back up and put it in my chest pocket. Alicia.

2 - RODENTS

It had been a full week since the first time Alicia hugged me. Now I planned my day around those few seconds when I might see her. I didn't have anywhere else to be, but I wanted to be sure I was at the station when she got off the subway. The note I held in my pocket said hugging me was the bright spot in her day. Somehow that made it feel like I had a responsibility, but it wasn't one that made me feel like running. Alicia needed a hug every day after work and I got to be the one to give it to her.

I had been thinking about things I had not been paying attention to for a long time. Like the fact that she had only seen me in the same set of clothes, and yet every time I saw her she looked fresh and pretty. It's probably okay that I wore the same jeans and jacket and maybe she didn't notice my shirt. I hoped she didn't think I smelled bad. I was thinking about all this when I passed a barber shop. I dreaded the thought of getting my hair cut and subjecting some barber to my gross nappy head, but now I was considering it. I peered inside and saw the barber sitting alone reading the newspaper. The fact that there was no one else in there gave me the courage to stick my head in the door and asked him how much for a haircut. "Fifteen bucks," he answered without looking up. If he had looked up, he probably would have said thirty. Fifteen bucks meant three days' worth of food, but I decided to go for it. Who knows when I might get another chance to get a haircut in privacy? I entered the door and he looked up and set his paper down.

I felt ashamed of myself, but I sucked it up because I knew I needed to get this over with. I sat in his chair and took off my hat and looked at him to see his response. He didn't look shocked; he just asked, "Are we taking it all off then?"

"Leave whatever you can. I realize there isn't much to work with."

He held up a dread on top and said "I can put some stuff in here that will loosen it up, but most of it will have to come off. I can leave about an inch on top."

"I'd appreciate that."

He started snipping off dreads and we both were silent. I watched the matted patches of hair fall to the ground and they reminded me of a bunch of little rodents. I wished they would scurry away, go hide in the corner or under some chairs. The man was a middle-aged black guy wearing what looked like a white lab coat over his clothes, and he seemed deep in concentration. He continued to work in silence, detaching the rodents from my scalp and tossing them to the floor. I watched quietly until I couldn't take it anymore, "So is this the worst you've ever seen?"

"What, this?" He laughed. "Man, I have been at this a long time. This ain't even that interesting. You know what I saw a few weeks ago? This dude came in who never had a haircut in his life! Seventeen years old and never had a haircut before – scissors never touched his head!"

"No shit? Why?"

"Dude was a Sikh, man. They ain't supposed to cut their hair. Dude unwrapped this turban thing and had hair down past his ass. His dad too!"

"What made him cut it?"

"His dad finally let him. They had been fighting about it forever, until one day he took a bunch of pills and tried to kill himself! Then his dad said, 'Okay, the hair can go.'"

"Really? Kill yourself over hair?"

"Well it ain't just that, man, it was the control thing his dad and his religion had over him. Funny – long hair used to mean freedom, but for this kid it was the opposite. His dad hugged him when it was done and it felt pretty intense up in here."

"Hugs can be potent."

"So can religion. So can father-son relations. So what's your story, man? How'd you get hair like this? Don't look intentional."

"I stopped taking care of myself."

"No shit. How come? You depressed?"

I had not thought about that question before and no one had asked me. In fact, this conversation with the barber was the longest anyone had spoken to me in months. I thought back over the past year and how I felt when Carlos had a family to go home to, and how I couldn't find a new job. I thought about how letting first Thomas and then Jeff move in had ended up kicking me out of my own place, and what a bad decision that was. I thought about how I walked around in a daze every day, just existing, killing time. "Yeah, I guess I was depressed," I answered.

"Well I hope you come out of it, my man. You're young, got your whole life ahead of you, and now you got a nice haircut. Hey, why don't you let me give you a shave since you're gettin' all cleaned up?"

I agreed and when he was done he turned me around and handed me a small mirror so I could see the back of my head. That's when I looked into the big mirror for the first time. I studied my reflection and was kind of surprised to see that I looked like myself. I expected some older guy to be looking back at me, a guy that looked like he had been living on the streets. Instead, I saw a young, decent-looking clean-cut Ray with light brown skin and dark hair I got from my Puerto Rican Mom, and the greenish eyes that my Irish Dad passed along. The outsides didn't match how I felt inside, and I was glad about that.

"Hey thanks, man." I paid the barber, shook his hand and left. I walked outside with a naked feeling, as if I lost my shield. I had become used to feeling invisible. I wondered if people might stare at me, but to my relief I was just another anonymous New Yorker walking down a busy street.

After my haircut I was hungry so I went to a busy fast-food place looking for scraps that people left on their trays. The thought of eating other people's food was really making me sick on this particular day, but I had already spent my food money. I finally couldn't take it and broke down for the cheap stuff on the value menu. I ate it but couldn't enjoy the lousy meal knowing I would run out of money before the month ended. I spent the rest of the afternoon at the library reading and charging my phone. I got a text from a high school buddy saying he would be coming to the city that weekend, but I didn't answer him. I really didn't feel like seeing anyone and explaining what I had been up to.

I arrived at the subway station at 5:00 and was glad Robbie wasn't there that day to make a scene or ask for money. When the 5:15 subway arrived I saw Alicia right away. She looked at me and smiled, then looked down all bashful-like. I watched her walking towards me and when she got close I held my arms open and she stepped into my embrace. I inhaled deeply and smelled her fresh hair. She backed up and was smiling, "Hey, you shaved!"

"Got a haircut too," I said, lifting my baseball cap to show her my groomed hair. Then I realized she never knew how bad it was having not seen me without my hat.

"Very clean-cut," she said. "It looks good."

"I liked your note. My name is Ray."

"Nice to meet you, Ray," she giggled and stuck out her hand. "Kinda' funny to shake your hand when we went straight to hugging each other."

"Well, I like hugging you too, Alicia." She smiled and looked down. She seemed very shy when it came to conversation, and that surprised me. She seemed so bold and brave to hug me in the first place. I didn't know what to say but I didn't want her to walk away so I teased her, "Do you always hug random strangers in subway stations?"

"Well, you kind of asked," she laughed. "Plus, I wanted to thank you."

"For what?"

"For helping me that day." I just stared at her blue eyes having no idea what she was talking about, so she went on, "Don't you remember? A few weeks ago the latch on my briefcase broke and everything spilled out and you didn't say anything, just got on your knees and started gathering up my papers? I never got a

19

chance to thank you because you took off so quickly."

"Oh yeah," I lied. The truth is I had no memory of it, but it wasn't out of character. I decided she would know better than me since I had been walking around in a haze.

"Well, I bought a new briefcase with a zipper after that."

"I can see that," I said. I wished I knew what to say next, but aside from talking to the barber that morning, I was really out of practice with conversation.

She stood there for a few seconds looking at me and looking away, then said, "Well, I'd better go. I have a class tonight."

"Okay. Bye, Alicia."

"Bye, Ray. See you tomorrow," and she walked away. She turned around after about twenty steps and waved. I waved back and said, "See ya'." I cursed myself for not talking more. Why didn't I ask what kind of class? Maybe it was good I didn't say too much. I could have easily blown it and at least I knew I would see her the next day.

I slept in my apartment that night and even took a shower. I stopped by in the evening to see if the guys paid their rent but it was empty and dark. I slept in my clothes on the couch and was woken by Thomas in the early morning. He looked like hell. He told me he paid his part of the rent but had not seen Jeff and that Jeff still needed to pay. He asked if he could have the couch and I gave it to him. Neither of us wanted to sleep on the cot and I couldn't sleep with him there anyway. It was almost 5:00 so I headed out to the donut shop.

I didn't drink coffee when I first moved to New York but

now I did. It's cheap and comes with refills and sometimes they even give it out for free at churches and stuff. Plus, it buys real estate. You can park in one spot for a long time with a cup of coffee and a book. I was reading a book called *Extremely Loud and Incredibly Close*, about this kid who loses his dad in one of the Twin Towers. It's a sad book but funny at times and I liked how the kid was a loner roaming all over New York by himself. I bought a donut and ate it, but I was still hungry so I bought a second. I was growing more concerned about the rate I was burning through my money these past two days and I knew I wouldn't make it to the end of the month.

At 8:30 I started walking back to the library knowing they open at 9:00. I wanted to hang out there and read and if I got there early I could sit in one of those comfortable chairs by a window. As I was walking down the street I see these two guys coming down a stoop carrying a fridge and the guy on the bottom was cussing and yelling so I stepped over and started helping him. We got the fridge set down on the ground and he thanked me and asked if I could help him get it into the back of the truck that was parked right there, so I said sure. Afterwards he brushed his hands off on his pants and looked me up and down and said "You workin'?"

I shook my head and said no.

"You want to work today? One of my guys didn't show up. It's just grunt work; we are clearing out this apartment. Some asswipe left it a sick mess. Pays a hundred bucks a day. Cash."

Did I want to make a hundred bucks? Hell yes, I did. I couldn't believe my luck! He introduced himself as Don and the other guy as Lenny and I shook both their hands. I followed Don and Lenny up the stoop, into the building, and up the stairs into a disgusting little apartment full of boxes and trash and a few pieces of beat up furniture, including a soiled mattress. "We gotta get all this crap outta here and get the walls ready to paint. Tomorrow I want to paint and have new fixtures in before the carpet gets put in. Landlord wants to show it this weekend." I couldn't imagine the place being habitable by then, but it wasn't my business. I just started helping carry things down to the truck. We got the big stuff out first and then there was a ton of little crap. It really was a stinky foul mess.

The hours went by really fast and I didn't say much but learned a lot about their business and their families by listening to Don and Lenny's conversation. There was an ease between them that led me to believe they had known each other a long time. Don owned the business and both men busted each other's balls a lot, but I noticed Don also asked Lenny's opinion on some work stuff. Both men seemed to be around mid-forties, but Don was stout with a pot belly and Lenny was tall and lanky. At one point Lenny left to take a load to the dump and when he came back he brought three turkey sandwiches. We sat out on the stoop to eat them and I tried to eat mine really slowly, so I wouldn't look like a ravenous pig. It was the best meal I had had in a long time.

Don asked me a few questions about what I had done for work in the past and I told him about my old job and how I worked for my dad's plumbing business. This got him really excited and he asked if I could remove the sink and toilet and I said sure, but I didn't have any tools. He laughed and said he had tools but hated plumbing, so I went into the bathroom and worked alone for a while. I noticed it was getting late and we still had a way to go. I started to think I wouldn't make it to the station by the time Alicia got there and I was getting really anxious until I realized that this was a rare chance for me to make some money. At least I knew where she would be the next day since she was pretty consistent, but I didn't want her to think I didn't want to be there. My mind went back and forth but I knew I needed to keep working and when five o'clock came we were finally done. There was no way I was going to make it to the station on time, but when

Don reached into his wallet and handed me a Benjamin, I knew I had done the right thing. Then he asked me if I could come back the next day and help put the new fixtures in and I said, "Hell yeah," and shook his hand.

I was disappointed I did not see Alicia, but felt almost euphoric over having some money in my pocket and the chance to make some more the next day. I decided I'd better go buy a pair of jeans and a shirt or two, but I didn't go crazy spending. Luckily I found some jeans on sale. I still ate off the value menu and sitting there it struck me that I had eaten three meals that day. I walked down the crowded sidewalk towards my apartment, feeling really odd. It almost made me uncomfortable to feel so different, like things were changing rapidly and I wasn't in control. I had interacted with more people in the past few days than in the several weeks prior. It felt overwhelming.

Arriving at my building, I was uncertain about going upstairs, not sure what I would find and if it would ruin this odd but peaceful state of mind I was experiencing. I knocked on Louisa's door and asked if she could wash my new clothes that night so I could wear them to work the next day. She said yes and gave me the okay to knock on her door as early as 6:00 a.m.

I went to my door and put my ear up to it, but did not hear anything. I decided to skip knocking and just use the key. Thomas was still on the couch passed out and Jeff was nowhere to be seen. There were beer bottles strewn all over the floor near Thomas and he smelled like piss. I decided to take a chance and sleep on the cot, hoping he would just sleep through the night. I set the alarm on my phone and kept it in my pocket and lay down with my clothes on and thought about Alicia. I wondered if she was disappointed I wasn't at the subway station to hug her. I hoped so.

When my phone alarm vibrated, I woke with a start

wondering where I was, then remembered I had slept in the apartment. I was surprised that I had slept so many hours in a row. Thomas was still passed out on the couch and I could smell the sweet-and-sour, putrid stench of alcohol and piss coming off him. I knew it was normal for him to stay up for days and sleep for days and I knew I did not want to be there when he woke up. I took a quick shower and even found some bottled soap in the medicine cabinet, but still had no towel. I retrieved my new clean clothes from Louisa and came back to change, being careful not to wake Thomas. I stopped at Louisa's one more time with my dirty laundry and she said, "Work hard, Ray." I agreed and meant it.

I still had time for coffee and a donut before making it back to the jobsite with plenty of time to spare. The apartment we were working on was empty now and Lenny started patching up the holes in the wall while I helped Don carry up a new bathroom sink and toilet. He asked me if I could hook them up and I said sure. It took a few hours and when I got done he had a garbage disposal for me to hook up and then I got to paint. I actually like painting but Don told me I was being too picky – that this wasn't the Taj Mahal. Yeah, no kidding. It was almost as sick as my place, just a little bigger and the windows faced the street instead of looking into someone else's apartment. At least it had new stuff in it now, but everything we put in was low-quality, cheap stuff. Don said in this rental bracket they just put in the cheap stuff knowing it would need replacing. Then he told me that sometimes they got to work on nice places and they had one next week on the other side of town.

I was worried that I wouldn't get to see Alicia that day, but we got kicked out of the apartment at 2:00 so that the carpet guys could do their thing, and Don told me I could come back the next day if I wanted. He still paid me a hundred bucks and I said it wasn't even a full day but he said the day before was extra long. Then he asked for my number saying he would text me about tomorrow.

I decided to get a hot dog and wait in the park until it got closer to 5:00. I watched some kids playing soccer, and I watched a lot of women pushing strollers, and I watched a lot of tourists, and I watched a lot of joggers. I read more *Extremely Loud* and decided to call my dad and tell him I had a job, even though I did not know how long it would last. I got his answering machine and told him there.

Finally it was five o'clock and I was at the subway station waiting for Alicia. I saw her before the doors opened. She saw me too and smiled and walked straight to my open arms. I hugged her a long time this time. Now that I knew she liked hugging me I felt less nervous about it and not so scared that it would never happen again. "I had to work late yesterday. Sorry I missed you," I said.

"Oh, I figured it was something like that."

"I want to walk you home."

She looked at me surprised and said, "I really don't know you that well, Ray."

"Yeah, but I want to get to know you."

"Well," she paused, "I don't want you to know where I live just yet."

That had not occurred to me, but it made sense. She really did not know me, so I appreciated the fact that she didn't know if I was a crazy guy or not. I also noticed she said "yet" and that made me happy.

"How 'bout just part of the way?" I asked.

She smiled and said that was a good idea and we walked out of the subway station. I offered to carry her briefcase, but she declined. I started asking her questions and she asked me some. I learned that she was two years older than me and that she had moved to New York from California less than a year ago. She worked in an office doing accounting in Greenwich Village, and that she was still going to school to become a CPA. She asked about me and I told her how I came to the city with Carlos and how we lost our jobs after a year but I stayed and that I just got a new job doing construction. I surprised myself at how normal I made my life sound. Alicia told me about her family, that her parents are still married and that she has two little sisters in California and that they would all be coming for a visit in a month. I told her about how my mom died during my senior year in high school and how I still missed her every day.

Then she stopped and showed me a picture of herself with her sisters on her phone. They were at the beach and they were all wearing swimsuits. The photo showed them from the waist up and Alicia looked really hot in her blue bikini top. She reached for the phone and I told her to hold up, that I wasn't done looking at it and she laughed, but I said I wasn't kidding.

"Text it to me."

"Really? No way, I couldn't do that."

I gave her my puppy dog look that used to work on my mom and Alicia said, "I'll send you a different one that doesn't have my sisters in it." I handed her the phone back and she asked for my number and texted me her graduation photo. She still looked beautiful, but of course she was all covered up and not in a bikini. But now I had her number and said so.

"Maybe I wanted you to have my number." She said it in a sassy tone, then smiled at me, and then she got that shy look I had come to recognize when her eyes dart around and she does this little shoulder shrug before speaking again. "We are pretty close to my place, but I want you to stop here. Okay?"

"Of course, Alicia. I want you to feel safe walking with

me, not uncomfortable."

She looked relieved and gave me my second hug of the day, a rather long one and I felt a real flush of protectiveness about her. I really wished I could walk her to her door, but I understood. She backed up and smiled at me sweetly and said, "Goodbye, Ray. I hope I see you again tomorrow."

"Well, if I can't make it on time, I can always call you."

"Yes, you can."

I watched her walk away and turn a corner and wanted to follow her but didn't. At least now I had a picture of her on my phone. And her phone number. I patted my phone through the pocket of my jacket and felt like the richest guy in New York City.

3 - COFFEE

I walked back to the apartment feeling the heat in the air and the warmth in my pocket. I now had Alicia's picture and phone number safely tucked away and I felt like I had a little piece of her with me. I reveled in the awareness of how much my life had changed recently, but I also had some pretty serious problems to deal with. Right now I needed to find out if Jeff paid his rent.

As I walked up our stoop, I saw Thomas gingerly coming down the steps, holding the railing looking like a skeleton wrapped in skin and dirty clothing. He had sunken eyes and scabs all over his face. A woman was holding his arm, but she didn't have the look of either a hooker or a drug addict. When Thomas saw me he said, "Hey, Ray. My mom's taking me to detox. I'll see you in a few weeks."

"Maybe not," his mom intervened, "Thomas might be going to a halfway house." Thomas shook his head at me while his mom looked me up and down like she didn't trust me.

"What about Jeff? Have you seen him? Did he pay his rent?" I asked.

"No idea," he answered, as he stepped into a waiting cab with his mom.

"Well, good luck, man," I hollered after him, stunned at this turn of events.

I didn't see any evidence that Jeff had been back to the apartment and I felt really stressed knowing that tomorrow was the end of our grace period. Adding to my anxiety was the worry that I didn't know if Jeff would bust in the door at any moment, or if he would be friendly or high or crazy or have company or what. I never knew what to expect and it kept me on edge. I looked around our crappy little apartment and wanted to bask in some solitude, but I couldn't hang there and relax in the state it was in. I decided to go down to the corner store and buy some cleaning supplies. Trying to stick to a budget, I bought trash bags, a roll of paper towels, a sponge and some cleanser. I also bought a pack of disposable razors and some milk and cereal.

When I got back, I decided to push the couch up against the door so I would have plenty of warning before someone came barging in. I found some good music on my phone and with the earplugs in was able to get into the cleaning groove. I bagged up beer bottles and trash and some nasty looking rags, porn magazines, cigarette butts, and more trash. I found two shirts that belonged to me but they were covered in some sticky substance I didn't want to deal with, so I threw them away. I found a pair of woman's shoes and one shoe that was mine. I tossed them all in the bag and closed it up and put it next to the couch and had a seat. I felt anger well up in me that I had to clean all this shit up, and that the rent wasn't paid, and that Thomas had a mom to help him. I was pissed that we lost our jobs and I had to live with these creeps instead of Carlos. I felt angry about the recession and how my dad had to deal with that crap while missing my mom at the same time. Then I got mad at myself for being angry, but I couldn't stop.

Just then my phone vibrated. My first thought was maybe it was Alicia, but it was my dad texting me saying, "Congratulations on the new job. Don't blow it." Somehow I took that as a sign to get off my ass and keep cleaning. A few minutes later I got a text from Don with the message, "Same location, 8:00."

I really didn't expect Alicia to text or call me. Now that I knew her a bit and how shy she could be, it seemed even more astounding that she hugged me in the first place. I looked at her picture several times while I cleaned until finally I was exhausted, and then I rewarded myself with the luxury of a long shower. The place looked a lot better, but I had not even touched the kitchen yet.

While I was in the shower my thoughts drifted back to Alicia and I was getting hard but I didn't want to think about her that way. Somehow it didn't seem right. Instead, I thought about the last time I had sex. It had been when Carlos was still living here. We met these two girls, brought them back to the apartment, and got drunk with them. We had to flip a coin to see who would get to stay in the main room and who would have to go in the bathroom. I ended up having sex with that girl in this tiny bathroom while I sat on the toilet and she sat on my lap.

We never saw them again because Carlos's girl told him she had a boyfriend. I wasn't that into mine anyway and they seemed kind of like a package deal. If I'd known it was the last time I'd be having sex for a really long time, I might have taken my time and tried to enjoy it more. I never would have expected that I wouldn't have the privacy to even consider sex, but now it seemed my dick was coming out of hibernation. I thought about that girl who sat on my lap, but it bummed me out that I didn't even remember her name.

After my shower, I looked at Alicia one last time and set the alarm on my phone and went to sleep on the couch while it was still in front of the door. Jeff never did make an appearance.

I woke up with a start. The grace period on our rent was up and I did not have the last third. Even with the remainder of my unemployment check and the money I earned from Don I was still short. I wanted to just go back to sleep and forget about it, but decided I'd better call the property managers rather than wait for one of those legal notices on my door. I told the girl on the phone that one of my roommates had to go to the hospital, which was technically true since Thomas went to detox. She told me I was supposed to have only one roommate anyway; any more and I'd be violating the lease agreement. I explained that I only had one roommate now. She gave me five more days since we had paid two thirds of the rent, but told me I had better stick to our agreement. I thanked her and sighed in relief.

When I got to work Don was standing in the apartment with a list for me. He was going to another job and told me to finish painting the bathroom, put all the cover plates back on the outlets, and hook up a kitchen faucet. He reminded me, again, this wasn't the Taj Mahal and gave me an address to go to when I finished. It felt really good that he trusted me to work alone. He even gave me the keys and told me to lock up when I was done and put the keys in a lockbox, so I put my headphones on and got to work.

That afternoon I met Don and Lenny at a really nice penthouse and it amazed me that there could be such a vast difference in lifestyle when the two places were a short walk apart. That is the crazy thing about New York: wealth and poverty are right on top of each other. This place had a view of Central Park and it was being remodeled. I had to wear paper booties on my shoes because the people still lived there and they had white carpet. That is something you would never see in a lower-rent place.

I helped Lenny remove kitchen cabinets that looked like they were brand new. Lenny informed me that they wouldn't go to a dump, that they had a place to sell them. While we were working I heard Don on the phone talking about how the guy who used to work for him tried to come back but he fired him. I heard him say, "Ray is worth two of him anyway. He shows up on time and keeps his mouth shut." It made me feel really good to hear him say that, although, truth be told, the mouth shut part was a matter of not having much to say. I used to be pretty outgoing and a joker back in school, but that felt like a lifetime ago.

When it got close to 4:00 I asked Lenny if he thought we would be working late, and he asked if I had somewhere to go. I told him I liked to walk my girl home from the subway, but I could work as late as he needed me. I amazed myself at how I had this new ability to deceive people without actually lying. Alicia wasn't my girlfriend but somehow calling her my girl seemed okay. Lenny said it was cool since he needed to be somewhere too. I had to run to the subway station to make it on time, but Alicia wasn't there.

I decided to text her. I wrote four different messages and erased them all, trying to come up with the right thing to say that didn't sound too eager or lame. While I was writing my fifth text, I got one from her that said "Hi, are you at the station?"

"Yeah," I texted back. "Where are you?"

"Just got on the train. Can you wait?"

"No prob." Alicia wanted me to wait for her. I tried to wipe the smile off my face then remembered I had a book in my pocket. I stood against the wall and started reading *Extremely Loud*.

I was almost to the last page and so into it I didn't even watch for the subway, but I heard Alicia say my name and she walked right into my arms. She actually put her hands inside my jacket and hugged me around my waist instead of my shoulders. This was new and I liked it. I really liked it.

"Have you heard that commercial on the radio where they say a hug reduces stress?" she asked.

"No, but I believe if for sure."

"Yes, but I was listening and it said a twenty second hug. That's a long hug, if you think about it. Twenty seconds!"

"I've got time. That would just be a warm up."

Alicia laughed like I was joking and didn't take me up on it. "Thanks for waiting for me, Ray."

"My pleasure. Is it okay if I walk with you for a bit?"

"I was hoping so. In fact, I was hoping you might have time to stop for a cup of coffee. Do you like coffee? I mean, a drink might be... Well, I have to study tonight." She looked nervous and I could really see how she went from confident to shy faster than anyone I had ever known and I liked both sides of her, but when she got anxious it made me feel more at ease.

"I love coffee," I answered.

"Oh, great! I mean, first I ask you to wait for me, then make you go to coffee with me."

"I love coffee," I said a second time. "You're not making me do anything. There is no place I'd rather be right now."

Alicia smiled at me and said "Okay then, let's go."

There was a coffee place on the way home that she liked,

and we walked there together as she told me about her study group and how she didn't do much besides go to school and work. She still felt new to the city and had a whole list of places she wanted to see. I told her that I have walked all over the island and know a lot of cool places but have not been to many of the tourist spots. I explained that I liked to read books that take place in New York and told her about the one I was reading now. I answered her questions about my job by telling her I was working on remodeling a kitchen in a nice penthouse, and that I really liked it and the guys I worked with seemed cool.

When we got to the coffee shop, Alicia ordered some type of latte and I just ordered a cup of coffee and tried not to choke when they told me the price. I was used to Dunkin Donuts, but this place did have a nice cozy atmosphere and tables with lamps. I made a mental note to come back here if I needed a place to hang out in the future.

The coffee shop was crowded, but we got lucky and a couple was just getting up from a small table by the window. Alicia sat down across from me and started sipping her coffee. It gave me a good chance to look at her while she talked. Of course I had studied her photo, but that was only one expression and Alicia seemed to have a million of them. She was so expressive I felt like I could be across the room and not able to hear and still know what she was talking about.

She apologized that she didn't have more time to hang out, but I was happier than she could fathom just to be sitting there with her. I didn't expect this to last or go anywhere. Sooner or later my façade of being a normal functioning person was going to fail me and she would see the truth, but right now I planned to just enjoy the company of a pretty girl who felt like talking to me. I was amazed at this new talent I had acquired for making my life sound so normal, telling her my roommate just moved out and he left the place a mess, just like it was any ordinary situation. If she only knew the guy she was sitting with slept outdoors and picked food out of the trash, I was certain she would run home at full speed.

Too soon Alicia was picking up her briefcase and asking if I wanted to walk with her part of the way. Of course I did.

"Do you have any plans for the weekend?" She asked.

"I play soccer every Saturday morning, but other than that, I figure I'll just try to get my apartment back in order."

Alicia didn't say anything and I started to feel like I might be blowing it. I know that asking me if I had plans was an opportunity to ask her out, but I couldn't. Yet I didn't want her to think I didn't want to. I decided I would rather risk her thinking bad about me than thinking I just don't like her, so I touched her arm and stopped her on the sidewalk. I gently moved her to the side so I could talk to her.

"Hey, Alicia, I guess you must know I like spending time with you. I really want to ask you on a proper date and take you to some of those places you want to see, like the Guggenheim, or something like that. Hell, I think it would be cool to tour the whole city with you. But there is something you don't know."

She looked at me expectantly and I went on. "You probably get asked out a lot, by guys who have a lot to offer and can take you to nice dinners and all that, and you should probably do that because I am not who you think I am."

"Who do I think you are, Ray?" She asked with her head tilted to one side.

"I don't know," I shrugged. "An ordinary guy capable of taking a girl on a date?"

"And you're not that?"

"Well, no. Not really. The truth is I've been unemployed for some time and I just lost my roommate unexpectedly and…. Well, I just got a job and am trying to get on my feet."

"There are a lot of things to do that don't cost money, Ray. If you wanted to walk through the park with me I would say yes."

"You would?"

"Yes."

"Really?"

"Yes." She was smiling at me and my mind was spinning. I wanted to believe her and I wanted to hang out with her, but it was making me feel really anxious anticipating what could go wrong. I couldn't feel good about hanging out with a girl and barely being able to buy her a hot dog from a cart. She deserved better than me and I said so.

"Alicia, you shouldn't waste your time with me. You probably have a bunch of guys asking you out all the time, guys who could buy you a nice dinner and take you cool places."

"Yeah, they're lining up outside my door. I think I got about twenty text messages just while we were having coffee," she laughed, then went on, "I'm kidding, Ray. The truth is I don't date much at all. I've been too busy with school to think about dating. Most guys wouldn't want to get involved with someone who has to study and go to class all the time. In fact, I have a study group early Saturday morning, but I can meet you at the park after your soccer game and we don't have to spend any money at all."

I answered her with a twenty-second hug.

I didn't want to go home to my empty apartment without a book to read, so I decided to hop on the subway and go to the Mid-Manhattan Library because they stayed open a lot later than the St. Agnes branch, plus it is a pretty cool place to hang out. I finished my book on the subway and it was so good I almost didn't want another book; I just wanted to think about this kid Oskar walking all over New York and missing his dad like I missed my mom. But I knew once I got back to the apartment I'd wish I had a book, so I went. I tried to return my book in the drop box, but it was all the way full with books sticking out of it so I walked up to one of the help desks and said "I'd like to return this but the drop is full."

The guy didn't look away from his computer screen and just said "Okay, leave it there and I'll take care of it."

I didn't want to so I said, "Can you check it in for me? I need to get another book."

"That won't be a problem. Just leave it there," he answered in an irritated tone.

"Look, man, I've never had a library fine and I don't want to take a chance that someone picks up this book, so can you just check it in for me?"

The guy looked up from his screen and stood looking pissed as hell, but then he looked at the book and his face changed. "I love this book," he calmly stated. He actually picked it up and held it to his chest and I figured he was probably gay, but I kind of understood how he felt about the book. It really was a good one. "Heavy boots," he said with a sigh.

"Yeah, I related to that term myself. I feel like I've been wearing heavy boots for a while now."

"What a lovable precocious protagonist. Tell me, did you

38

enjoy the shift in point of view?"

"How it went back and forth to the Grandma's story? Honestly, not as much. I mean I felt like I should take it serious because she was a persecuted Jew, but the truth is I rushed it because I wanted to get back to Oskar's story."

"I share your feeling of contrition, but Oskar was such a charismatic character."

"Yeah, I feel like I'm actually going to miss him. I liked how he was all over New York, on foot and subways too."

"Manhattan is my mistress. Would you like me to recommend other books in this setting? It is one of the things I relish most about this vocation."

"Sure," I answered, curious about why a guy would want to be a librarian. "What else is cool about this job? Do you make good money?"

"Oh no," he laughed. "I am a bibliophile and a lothario. Consequently, this is my Eden."

"You're a what and a what?"

The librarian laughed and leaned in to say, "I love books and I love women, so I am like a kid in a candy store."

"Oh, I get it. I didn't guess that you love women."

"My vocation, speech, and impeccable dress support the impression that I might be homosexual, but that is of no concern to me. It can, in fact, be used to my advantage. Speaking of stereotypes, you probably wouldn't guess that 17% of all librarians are in fact male."

"No, I would not have guessed that."

"Have you read *Let the Great World Spin*, or *The Adventures of Cavalier and Clay*, or *The Tale of an American Dream*? Surely you've read *Catcher in the Rye*?"

"*Catcher in the Rye* more than once, but I'd read it again."

"Oh no, I think *Let the Great World Spin* would be an eminently sagacious selection after *Extremely Loud*. Perhaps you should take *Cavalier and Clay* since the other is so concise."

"And sagacious is a good thing?"

"Indeed."

"Are you able to schmooze a lot of women with that vocabulary?"

"Raymond, I am interacting on a daily basis with New York's finest array of literate women. It behooves me to impress the ladies with my vernacular."

"Hmmm. How did you know my name?"

"I just checked in your book and have located the two we discussed. I have already messaged one of the volunteers to bring the books to the desk for you."

"Wow, thanks. You are efficient. I go by Ray, by the way."

"William." He offered his hand and gave a firm shake. "I am confident you will enjoy these books, Ray. I have a talent for selecting literature. In fact, it has garnered me great prestige among the patrons."

Just then a very pretty brunette brought two books up to the desk and cheerfully offered, "Here you go, William. Do you need anything else?"

"That is all for now, Melissa." The girl looked disappointed and walked away. Just then two older women walked by and said, "Hi, William!" and waved.

"Ladies," William dipped his chin.

"Wow. You really are the big fish in this pond."

William leaned in and whispered in a very different tone, "Dude. You have no idea." Then winked and said goodbye.

When I got back to my apartment there was no sign of Jeff. I decided to buy a new lock for the front door tomorrow. Now I had two library books I didn't want to carry around and my new clothes that I got back from Louisa. It seemed pretty ridiculous that someone would steal things like that, but everything I owned had disappeared before. I couldn't even find a spoon for my cereal and had to take a plastic utensil from a fast food place.

I set about cleaning up the kitchen. The fridge was disgusting, even though there was no real food in there, just a bottle of catsup. I found some weird shit in the cabinets that I didn't know what to do with. There were a bunch of random handwritten notes that didn't make any sense, a lot of radio and computer parts, and even two cheap watches. I didn't know if I should throw the stuff away in case one of the guys came back, but then I thought, *Fuck them!* and dumped it all in the trash. I was surprised to find a few tools, screwdrivers, and a wrench, so I started a tool drawer. I took a break on the couch, which I had once again pushed to block the door. I really wanted to text Alicia, but I didn't want to blow it by being overanxious when I had seen her just a few hours ago. But I did it, I couldn't resist. I texted "Try not to think about me too much."

I regretted sending it instantly, until I saw her reply a few

41

minutes later: "I'm trying" with a smiley face. Then I was glad I did.

4 - STRAWBERRIES

I woke to the sound of a key turning in the lock, then the deadbolt turning. Jeff was back. The knob turned, but he couldn't open the door because of the small latch-hook on the inside of the door. And there was the matter of the couch blocking the door as well.

He started banging on the door, "Thomas? Ray? Open up! It's me." I relocked the two locks and didn't answer.

"What the fuck? Open the goddamned door!" He banged louder. "Thomas! Ray! Open the motherfuckin' door!" He unlocked the door again and I saw the knob twist. Then he started banging on the door. "Open up!"

"Go away, Jeff. You didn't pay, you can't stay here

anymore," I yelled through the door.

"Ray! You better open this fucking door right now or I'm gonna kick your ass!"

I felt surprisingly calm as I locked the door again. I did feel irritated that he was keeping me awake when I had a game in the morning, but I wasn't all that worried that he would get in. But then he started kicking again.

"Ray! Open the door! Now!" he yelled.

I didn't answer and turned on the light. I made up my mind that if he came through that door I was going to kick his scrawny drug-addict ass. I was sick of his shit and there was no way he was going to stay here ever again. Anger started to well up in me as I wondered why I ever let him intimidate me in the first place. Just because he was loud and crazy didn't make him tough. Hell, I started to hope he would bust through that door and I hoped he tired himself out in the process. I stood there with my fists clenched, staring at the door as he continued to kick and kick, yelling at me to open up. I could see one of the screws on the latch was protruding and the wood trim on the door was starting to split. It seemed like time was passing really slowly and I wondered why he had not busted through yet. My senses were heightened and I was imagining the feeling of my fist connecting with his face, what that would feel like. I felt myself swelling with anger, a feeling I had been ignoring for a long time and now Jeff was about to give me my opportunity to put it to good use. Fear had completely left me and I felt like a wild animal ready to pounce the second he came through that door. Jeff kept yelling and hammering his foot against the door, ranting about kicking my ass, and I was ready to get on with it. I was getting so impatient I was about to open the door just so I could shut him up once and for all, but then it got suddenly quiet. I heard some mumbling and then a loud rap on my door followed by "NYPD! Open up."

It didn't sound like Jeff, but I wasn't certain so I moved the couch and unhooked the latch. As I opened the door a crack I saw a badge. The cop asked me if I lived there, what my name was, and then asked me to hand over my ID. I didn't see Jeff, but the cop told me his partner was questioning my friend and he wanted my version of what was going on.

I told him Jeff used to stay there but he had not paid his rent and I wasn't going to let him stay anymore. He asked whose name was on the rental agreement and I told him me and Carlos. He asked if I had ever been arrested and I answered truthfully, "No." He took my ID and excused himself for a minute while he stepped outside.

I sat down on the couch and waited but it was way longer than a minute. I wasn't worried about what would happen to me, but I wanted Jeff gone. After about fifteen minutes the cop returned and gave me my ID back. "Okay, Raymond, you checked out fine, but your friend won't be back anytime soon." He ran his hand over the wood trim and I asked about Jeff, "Did you arrest him for trying to break in?"

The cop laughed and said, "No, he didn't actually get in, did he? All he did tonight was disturb the peace. A few of your neighbors called it in, but he had warrants and some prescription drugs on his person that don't belong to him. They belong to a woman who got mugged yesterday. He was too stupid to ditch the bottle."

"Whoa, really? I knew he was a creep, but that's pretty bad."

The cop laughed and said, "Yeah, really bad for him. He's a creep alright. Tried to tell us he bought the pills off someone else, but he matches the description, and there were witnesses." He pulled out a card with his name and number and said goodnight as he headed out the door.

I put the couch back in front of the door out of habit and flopped down. I turned the light out and tried to sleep but found that I couldn't. There was too much adrenaline flowing through me from getting ready for the fight that never happened. Plus, I was hungry as hell, so I ate the rest of my cereal, drank all my milk, and thought about Jeff getting booked in jail.

I read until the sun came up and felt really amped up about my game and the anticipation of seeing Alicia afterwards. Louisa gave me my clean soccer shirt and shorts and also my clean t-shirts so I could put one on after the game. I asked Louisa if she had a grocery bag so I could carry my spare shirt in it and she said, "You can't walk around with a grocery sack full of clothes! You wanna look like a bag lady?"

"No, ma'am, I sure don't," I laughed, happy that I actually cared.

"Hold on a minute." Louisa closed the door and returned a minute later and handed me a black backpack. "Use this. Give it back when you're done."

"Wow, really? Thanks, Louisa. I don't even have to wear my jacket now, I can keep my stuff in here."

"You look stupid in that jacket when it's so hot outside." I laughed and thanked her again. She was right, after all.

"Play hard, Ray."

I walked to the park, stopping for coffee on the way, and also got a bagel. I'd need some energy to play soccer and bagels cost more than donuts, but they seem to last longer. Arriving at the great lawn I saw Marcus and the other guys warming up. Marcus's wife was there with their two kids and she told me she had a Gatorade for me. Marcus patted my back and asked about Carlos. I admitted, "I need to call him."

I didn't expect to see Alicia for a while. She sent me a text saying she would be there around 11:00 and I texted her back saying, "Just look for the Hispanic guy in a soccer uniform," which was a joke because there would be about a hundred guys in the park fitting that description. Alicia texted back "I'll be the cute blonde in black sunglasses," which I thought was pretty sassy of her.

I got into the game and didn't start looking for her until the second half. Eventually I saw that cute blonde in sunglasses. She wasn't kidding. I had never seen her in casual clothes and she looked so young and incredibly cute I felt like tackling her, but I just waved and she waved back. She was wearing jean shorts that were truly short with a sleeveless yellow top and flat sandals. Her hair was up in a tousled, more casual way and she had big black sunglasses on. I shot a few glances her way, but mostly stayed focused on the game.

I am sure I turned it up a notch knowing Alicia was watching me and dug deep in my reservoir to go after the ball – or maybe it was a rush of testosterone – but I had a good game. I got to tackle twice and even showed off with a scissor move. We ended up losing 3-2, but I was about as happy as could be. Alicia was talking to Marcus's wife when I walked up and I didn't want to hug her because I was too sweaty but she hugged me anyway and I didn't stop her.

"That was so awesome! You're really good, Ray! Gloria was just telling me about how you and your friend Carlos totally improved the team!"

I felt a combination of pride and embarrassment as she said that. I was ashamed of myself that I didn't know Marcus's wife's name before that moment and here she was bragging about me to Alicia. "Oh yeah, we were the youngest on the team. We had a lot of energy back then."

"You still do! It was so cool to watch how fast you are." Alicia was smiling, I was smiling, even Gloria was smiling, and it was a little bit too much for me until Marcus came along and smacked me on the back and called me a show-off. Gloria handed me a bottle of Gatorade and I thanked her and sat down on the grass next to my backpack to drink and stop sweating.

Alicia sat down too and kept talking to Gloria. I was blown away at her ability to make small-talk with strangers. She had already learned the names of their kids and how old they were. I could tell that my pretty friend was making a big impression on both Gloria and Marcus. On me too.

After Marcus and Gloria gathered up their belongings and their kids and said goodbye, Alicia asked if we could sit in the shade. She had a backpack too and took out a thin blanket for us to sit on. It wasn't very big so our feet hung off. "Are you hungry? I brought food."

"You didn't have to do that." I felt embarrassed thinking she brought food because she knew I was broke.

"Well I thought you might be hungry after your game, and I'm hungry too and kind of a picky eater," she laughed.

"Well, I'm always hungry, but especially after playing soccer."

Alicia started taking food out of her backpack. She started with a container of strawberries, grapes, crackers and cheese, and then she pulled out a sandwich that was on a bagel. But it was the strawberries that blew my mind. They were so sweet and juicy. I honestly couldn't remember the last time I had eaten fresh fruit and I said so, "I guess I've been eating like crap for some time now. These strawberries are amazing."

"Well, you are lucky you play soccer and are super fit. But it is really important to eat right, you know."

"Believe me, I know. But it is easier said than done. Now that my roommate is gone I can probably start keeping food in the apartment and not eat fast-food crap."

"I never eat fast food. I take my lunch to work with me." Alicia insisted the sandwich was for me but that didn't make sense after she said she was hungry, but she said she had already eaten hers. "So, are you up for exploring the park with me?" she asked.

"Sure." I stood and pulled off my soccer shirt and swapped it with the clean t-shirt in my pack. Alicia stood up and started putting things back in her backpack and it gave me an opportunity to study her from behind. She had toned muscular legs that that led to a nice rounded butt and a small waist. I was really admiring the curve to her ass when she turned around. I think she caught me staring, but if she did, she didn't say anything. She held a sheet of paper in her hand and said, "Let's go."

As we started walking, Alicia told me she found information online about all the things to see in Central Park and that it would take days to see everything, so we could just focus on the mid-section since that is where we started. "For example, did you know the great lawn used to be the city's reservoir? It was drained in 1937." Alicia suddenly blushed and looked embarrassed. "I hope you don't think I'm a dork for looking all this up."

I laughed and told her I thought it was cool that she was excited about the city and no, I didn't know that about the reservoir.

"Oh good. Well then, you wouldn't know that they failed to remove part of the reservoir wall underground and it created drainage problems and the grass wouldn't grow. In the nineties they had to tear it all up."

I laughed again and said, "No, you're right. I didn't know that fact either. But what I do want to know is why you're an accountant and not a teacher."

Alicia laughed and said accountants make a lot more money. "But it isn't just that. I like accounting because... Well... You can solve every problem. There isn't any mystery or ambiguity. If something doesn't balance, I can always figure it out. Accounting makes sense and it is a puzzle I can solve."

"So you don't do well with uncertainty?"

"No. Sorry, I guess that makes me sound kind of rigid and not very appealing, but I like order. I like answers. I like black and white."

"Nothing wrong with that, I guess."

"Hey, have you ever been inside the Belvedere Castle?"

"No, have you?"

"No, but I really want to check it out!" Alicia was as excited as a little kid and she really seemed a lot younger in her shorts and sandals. She was walking quickly and saying, "Come on, Ray!" while I was purposely lingering to get another look at her ass and legs from behind.

I was relieved to find out it didn't cost any money to get in the Castle, but then I started to wonder if Alicia really gave a shit about this stuff or was just doing it because it was free, for my sake. She seemed enthusiastic, and I really hoped she wasn't being phony.

Inside, the castle was small and crowded. There was a "flora and fauna" exhibit about things that lived in the park that I thought was cool; we would have hung out there a long time if it weren't so congested. We stepped outside onto one of the balconies to get some air. We were pretty high up with a great view of the park, and Alicia started pointing things out to me like the Delacorte Theater and the Ramble. She was talking all bubbly and going on and on, but I wasn't listening that well. I was studying her lips and thinking about what it would be like to kiss her, but she interrupted that thought by saying, "Let's take a picture!" She took out her phone and pressed the button for a selfie and held her face right next to mine. Our cheeks were actually touching and she took the picture and said "Oh, it came out great! And look at the skyline in the background! Don't worry, Ray, I won't put it on Facebook."

"It didn't even cross my mind to worry about that, but I do want you to text it to me."

"You don't mind if I put it on Facebook?"

"No, why would I?"

"Oh, I don't know. Psychotic ex-girlfriend maybe? Or you don't want to be… Oh, I don't know, lots of reasons."

"Alicia, I have not even looked at Facebook in over a year."

Alicia's face froze. "You are joking, right? Ray, are you serious?"

"Yeah, I'm serious. I was never that into it anyway, but I haven't even looked at it since… I can't remember."

Alicia gazed at me with big eyes for a second, before going on, "That is how I communicate with all my friends back in

California. Don't you keep in touch with your friends from back home?"

"I haven't felt like it."

She looked at me with a blank stare and waited.

"Look, Alicia, when I moved to New York things started out really great for me, but then everything went bad. I just don't have much to brag about and that is what Facebook feels like to me – everyone saying look at me and how great I'm doing, and I haven't had anything to say."

"I get it, Ray. I have to take breaks from it once in a while too, but a whole year..?"

"Well, I've just been surviving up until recently. That hardly seems like a cool post. 'This is Ray, barely squeakin' by in the big city."

Alicia laughed and said, "Yeah, if Maslow wrote his 'hierarchy of needs' today, he would probably put 'Update Facebook status' on the third or fourth level."

I laughed and made a mental note to look up this Maslow guy because I really didn't know what she meant.

"Oh hey, look! Our photo already has four 'likes' and one comment. My friend Janet said 'Who's the hottie and does he have any friends?'" I laughed and realized I liked being called a hottie, but no, I don't have any friends. Not a single one.

Alicia put her phone away and looked at the paper she printed out about the park and asked if I wanted to walk through the Ramble. Of course I did. I would have agreed to just about anything. As we squeezed back through the crowded castle I took her hand so we wouldn't get separated and I didn't let go when we got out. Alicia didn't let go either.

We walked for a while, silently, and I didn't mind that. I liked the Ramble because it is like being in the woods and you could forget you are even in the city surrounded by millions of people. I am always surprised that so few people go through there. Then I started worrying if she was having fun. I like it quiet sometimes and hoped Alicia did too, but she had been quiet for a while, maybe thinking. Hopefully not questioning what she was doing here with me. Finally she broke the silence. "Ray, I really think you should check your Facebook."

I laughed in relief upon hearing the reason for the serious expression, but asked, "Why does it matter?"

"Maybe you missed something important. Besides, your life isn't all that bad right now. You played an awesome game of soccer, it is a beautiful summer day, and now you are seeing the sights with me. I think that sounds like an awesome day!"

"Well, I completely agree with that, but I don't see what Facebook has to do with anything."

"I want to send you a friend request and I don't even know your last name."

"Kelly."

"Really? Kelly?"

"What, did you expect 'Sanchez' or something? I'm half Irish."

"That explains the green eyes."

We were now deep into the maze of trees that make up the Ramble and I stopped Alicia on the trail and looked at her. "I'll check my Facebook page – but on one condition."

She looked up at me and I said, "I want our first kiss to be in the Ramble." Alicia's eyes got big and she asked, "Now?"

I nodded my head and put my hand on the side of her face and lowered my face right up to hers and for a second I didn't kiss her; I just looked in her eyes until she closed them, and I met her lips with mine, once very softly, once a bit more firmly, then once a lot longer. I backed my head up, not wanting to be too greedy right away, looked her in the eyes, and said, "I've wanted to do that for a long time."

"Me too," she answered in a soft voice. Then she took my hand and started walking again. We walked all through the Ramble, and sat down and talked a few times, and walked around some more and talked awhile. Alicia took a few scenery shots with her phone. When we got back to the lawn she put her blanket under a tree and we sat down. I was fighting the urge to kiss her again. I didn't want to be too pushy, but now that I had tasted those lips I wanted more.

She told me she had to go a party that night for a coworker, a cocktail party that was a bridal shower, and said they didn't have those types of showers in California. She felt kind of awkward about going, but she had a friend from work to hang out with there.

I knew that our time together was coming to an end and I wanted to make plans to see her again, but I still had the problem of lack of funds. "Want me to check my Facebook now?" I asked, not because I wanted to, but because I didn't want to say goodbye.

"Yes!"

Alicia leaned her head on my arm as I took my phone out and tried to remember how to do it. I didn't have that little icon on my phone and had to go through the Internet. As soon as I did Alicia squealed, "Oh my god, Ray, you have 94 notifications!"

I was surprised as well. "I have a friend request from a guy I know from school, and a cousin, and oh, look at this cutie named Alicia Klaer. I'll have to take a closer look at her later."

I started scrolling through my page and aside from a bunch of old Happy Birthday messages, I saw a few friends from school saying "Hey Ray, gonna be in the city, let's get together," or "Hey man, long time, how've you been?" One guy tagged me in a few old photos and then there were more and more of "Where've you been, how've you been, tried to call you." It went on like that for quite some time, but the one that really caught my attention was from a cousin who said, "Thought of your mom today. I know she'd be proud of you." I noticed the post was on my mom's birthday.

I stopped reading and set the phone down on my thigh and I didn't want to say anything because I was feeling overwhelmed. I finally looked at Alicia and was startled by the fact that she had tears in her eyes.

"People miss you, Ray. A lot of people miss you."

"I had no idea."

"Where have you been?"

That was a tough question so I took my time before answering, "Checked out. I've been a walking zombie, Alicia. I've only been thinking about myself and what I was going through. Now I really feel like shit. But a really lovable piece of shit." We both laughed at that and I told her, "Your hug kinda' woke me up."

"You were like Sleeping Beauty?" She laughed.

"No, more like a guy with his head up his ass who let his problems overwhelm him."

"Well, you did have a tough year from what you've told me."

"Yeah. But that's no excuse. I'm gonna answer some of these people. Not all at once, or anything, but, you know..."

"I can tag you in that photo. You look pretty happy in that picture and people will know you are doing okay."

"Yeah, cool. Time to join the living, I guess. My friends will want to know who the hottie is and does she have any friends."

Alicia laughed and put her head back on my shoulder. "I have to go, you know."

"I know."

"I don't want to, but I have to. My coworker is meeting me back at my apartment."

"Can I walk you home?"

"Yes, please."

I walked Alicia all the way to her stoop and found out she lived on 83rd close to the park and only a few blocks from me. "What are you going to do tonight?" she asked as she turned around on the stoop.

"Bask in the solitude of my apartment."

Alicia got a pained look on her face and I said, "Really, you have no idea what a luxury it is to finally have the place to myself. I'm going to read and do some stuff at home. Probably spend a few hours on Facebook." I was joking about that part.

Alicia laughed and said, "I had a really good time today."

"Me too." She was standing on a step above me, which put

her face almost level with mine, and she already had her arms around my neck. I leaned in and kissed her lips, a long lingering kiss that I didn't want to end.

"Um, tomorrow?" she asked.

"Yes."

"I didn't even ask anything yet," Alicia laughed.

"Well, the answer is yes."

Alicia laughed again and said "It is my only day to sleep in, but can I call you when I get up?"

"I already told you: yes," and I kissed her again.

5 – NON-FAT-SUGAR-FREE LATTE

I woke up early Sunday morning feeling content and well rested. Sleeping in one place through the whole night was definitely having a good effect on me. I was feeling really good about how my life was changing, when just a few weeks ago I could not even imagine how to get out of the mess I was in. I found a job without looking, just walking down the street. I met an amazing girl while I was hanging out in the subway station acting like a goof. The weather was warming up and so was my life. I decided to walk outside, even though I had no particular place to go, a feeling I was very familiar with.

I like that there are fewer people on the streets on Sunday mornings compared to other mornings, but there are always people buzzing around at any hour. New York never takes a break.

The Catholic church up the street had just ended their early Mass and people were spilling out onto the sidewalk. I stopped to watch them clear out and then decided to go inside. It was the first time I had walked into that church without looking for a place to rest or get out of the weather. Instead, this time I wanted to light a candle for my mom and say thanks for my job and Alicia. Then I remembered Thomas and Jeff and while I did say a quick prayer for Thomas in detox, I also said "Fuck Jeff" under my breath. I'm no saint.

I stood up to leave and a little old lady started calling in a really loud half-whisper, "Young man, young man! Wait just a minute!" She really was tiny, like a miniature person wearing extremely fashionable clothes. In fact, as she tilted her head up at me, she looked like a little doll. A little old doll. "Excuse me, young man, what is your name?"

"Ray," I answered, and stuck out my hand. She took my hand in both of hers and clutched it.

"And how old are you, Ray?"

"Twenty-two."

"And do you have a girlfriend?"

I laughed and answered, "Well, there is a special girl who has come into my life recently."

"Dammit!" She exclaimed, right there in church, which made me instantly like her. "I was hoping to introduce you to my granddaughter. All the good ones are taken, just like she says! A good Catholic boy, no less."

"Oh, I'm no good Catholic," I laughed. I was all about misleading people these days, but I had to draw the line somewhere.

"Now see, just the humility of saying so tells me you are a nice boy. Besides, I saw you praying over there."

"I was just saying thanks for a few things. It's not like I was saying the rosary or anything."

"A prayer of sincere gratitude is worth more than a thousand rosaries," she smiled at me still holding my hand. "Now, tell me Ray, are you going over to the rummage sale?"

"No, wasn't planning on it."

"Well, would you walk me over there? I have trouble with the stairs."

"Sure," I answered and offered my arm even though she seemed to get around just fine. She held on tight to my arm and led me to the adjacent building and down into the basement. The church was having what looked like one giant garage sale. Garage sales are really not my thing, but I spotted a bunch of books on a table with a sign saying 25 cents each for paperbacks. I said goodbye to the little lady and started perusing the book collection. I looked up and around and noticed that the people didn't look half bad. I thought a rummage sale meant a lot of trash and there would be scroungy people there, but the crowd looked pretty normal. Except for the homeless guy standing next to me checking out the book collection. He smelt like piss and he was going through the box of books with serious determination. I know the feeling. When you don't have any place to store the books, you need to find one really good one.

"This one's good," I handed him a book I had in my hand that I had already read about this fat guy who rides his bike all over looking for his schizophrenic sister. It's called *The Memory of Running*, and I really wanted to reread it myself, but I wanted him to have it too. I handed him a dollar and told him he should read it and it was on me.

I picked out eight books for myself, reasoning that two bucks wasn't much to spend. Then I noticed a bunch of kitchen stuff on another table and remembered I didn't have any utensils at home. I couldn't believe how cheap everything was. The utensils didn't match, but I bought ten for a dollar. Next I noticed the clothing. Never in my life did I imagine I might wear someone else's clothes, but a pair of work boots caught my eye and I changed my mind. There was a lot of crap there too, but also some perfectly good items mixed in. I even found some jeans with the tags still on them.

I ended up walking out of that rummage sale with a whole box full of stuff for just under twenty dollars and it felt like Christmas morning. However, it was now ten o'clock and I had not heard from Alicia. I went home and started putting my stuff away and dropped the clothing off to Louisa for washing. Then I called my dad and told him that I still had a job. We never have much to talk about and I wanted to tell him about Alicia, but I thought I should keep it to myself in case it didn't last. I didn't tell my dad anything about what happened with the roommates or not paying my rent. It is a good thing my dad is not a big talker because I wanted to be off the phone when Alicia called.

I started to read a little bit, but I didn't feel like staying inside the apartment and I was hungry. I went out and bought a few groceries for the first time in a really long time. The strawberries looked enticing and my mouth started watering as I remembered how good they tasted the day before, but they were expensive, so I bought apples instead. I bought some food I could make at home like beans, rice, and pasta. Also some peanut butter, bread and jelly. It felt weird spending all that money at once, but now that I didn't have to worry about either roommate stealing my food, I knew this was the cheaper way to go in the long run. I checked my phone again and it was after eleven o'clock with still no message from Alicia.

Thinking back to our conversation, I was sure she said she'd call me when she woke up. How late could that girl sleep?

Maybe she wasn't going to call. Maybe she had second thoughts about hanging out with a guy with no money. Maybe she didn't like the way I kissed her. Maybe she met someone last night when she was out having cocktails. Maybe she realized what a piece of crap I am.

I made myself a sandwich and ate it as I was walking out the door. I still had Louisa's back pack and now I had an apple and a book in it as I headed to the park. I felt really light without my jacket, but my mood was heavy. Some guys were kicking a ball around and I watched them for a while. It made me think of Carlos and, since I had been meaning to call him, I did. I got his answering machine and said, "Hey, man, it's me, Ray. I know it's been a long time. Just wanted to see how you are doing. Gimme a call."

I was starting to feel really nervous about Alicia. It was after twelve o'clock and I was tempted to text her. Maybe she lost her phone. Nah, she figured me out: it was over. I was glad I got to kiss her though. I could think about that for a long time even if I didn't get to do it again.

My phone vibrated with a text, "I'm up! Call me when you can."

I smiled and got anxious all at once. "Call me when you can?" What does that mean? Does she think I'm busy and might not call her right away? I should be busy. I should have a life and be doing things on Sunday. Aw, fuck it, I'm calling her. I'll just wait a minute or two.

"Good Morning," she answered.

"Hey, how are you?"

"Good. I'm just waking up. I was up pretty late last night."

"Was it fun?"

"Um, yes and no," she said.

"How come?"

"Well it started out kind of fun, but I'm not used to drinking like that and it just went on and on and I felt kind of trapped. I didn't want to be the first one to leave because I am trying really hard to fit in there, but I ended up drinking more than I'm used to. Now I'm paying the price this morning."

"Ah," I said, not really sure what to say next. It had been a long time since I overindulged on alcohol. There was silence for a few awkward seconds, and then she said, "What are you up to this morning?"

"Oh, I'm just sitting at the park and eating a sandwich, watching some guys kicking a soccer ball around."

"Do you want company?"

"Only if it's you."

"Aww,... Can you give me an hour? I have to take a shower."

"You got it. Text me when you are close and I'll meet you."

"Okay, see you soon."

"Bye."

My mood skyrocketed. Alicia was going to hang out with me again today, but what could we do? She couldn't be happy just walking around the park again, but I didn't have any ideas. I decided to get some coffee and figure out exactly how much money I had left and how much more I needed to make my rent.

At a coffee shop across from the park I sat down and borrowed a pen from a lady at the next table. I did the math on a napkin. If Don kept me working for the next three days and paid me cash, I could pay the balance of the rent by the new due date and would have sixty-five dollars left over. That seemed like plenty and I relaxed a bit. I couldn't go crazy, but I could spend a few bucks. I took my book out and started to read until my phone vibrated and Alicia said she was walking up 83rd Street. We agreed to meet on the corner of 83rd and CPW. It occurred to me that I should bring her a latte.

Alicia came walking towards me wearing a summer dress and sandals. I love when a girl can pull off different styles and Alicia definitely has different flavors. Today she looked sunshine, all soft and pretty with her hair down. I saw her face light up when she saw me and it made me feel warm. She walked right into my arms like a heat-seeking missile. When she backed up I handed her the cup of coffee and she said, "Wow, thank you!" Then her eyes got big and she asked, "Is there sugar in it?"

"No, I ordered it like you did. Nonfat, no sugar."

"I can't believe your remembered how I take my coffee! That is so sweet!" She was smiling from ear to ear.

"It's no big deal, Alicia."

"Well, thank you," she smiled again and took a sip.

"You look really pretty today."

Alicia answered, "Thank you," as if she wanted to say more and bit her lip and swallowed. I got the impression it took some restraint for her to just accept a compliment. It was just a feeling I got, but she seemed uncomfortable as if she had to learn to just say thank you. I wondered if she didn't know how pretty she is.

"So, can we go back to the park?" She asked, excitedly. "There is a free concert at the SummerStage."

Damn, she said that word "free" again, a word I both loved and hated. The word that means "I know you're a broke loser." But of course I said okay – what else could I say? No, let's find someplace to spend my last sixty dollars? Alicia told me it was near Ramsey Playfield, a bit of a walk, but there was no easy way to get there aside from walking. I am used to walking and she insisted she loved walking but I found myself slipping into a low feeling. We walked side by side with Alicia sipping her coffee and me not saying anything.

Finally Alicia spoke, kind of coyly, "Sooooo, have you checked your Facebook?" She was grinning.

I laughed, "Forgot all about it."

"Ray," she punched me lightly in my upper arm, "How can I flirt with you on Facebook if you don't even check it?"

I laughed again and said, "I guess you'll have to flirt with me in person."

She stuck out her bottom lip and put her hand on her hip, so I said, "Okay, okay, I'll check it."

We stopped walking and stepped out of the way and I checked my page but didn't see anything from her. "Nope, nothing from that cute Alicia Klaer, but a few people like our photo."

"You have to click on my page! Jeez, Ray, I guess I don't have to worry about you being a cyber-stalker," she laughed.

"Yeah, I should have thought about that. Damn, all this time I've been waiting for your text I could have been looking at all your photos?"

"You were waiting for my text?"

"You know I was."

I had her page on my phone now and wasn't really sure what I was supposed to be looking for. "Look at my comment under our photo," she said.

I saw the comment from her friend calling me a hottie and underneath Alicia commented, "You should see him with his shirt off!" I laughed and thought it was just a joke but then I remembered that I changed out of my soccer jersey in front of her. "Hey, you were checking me out?" If I had thought about it at the time I probably would have worried that I had gotten too skinny this past year.

"Yeah," Alicia cocked a hip and looked me up and down. "I was checking you out. And I caught you checking me out too."

"Oh, I'm not denying it. You didn't need to shed any clothing to get my attention." I noticed Alicia was turning red and I was thinking how funny she was like that, going from bold to shy in an instant. I guess I am like that too because I just went from feeling like a broke loser to a sexy stud in a matter of seconds. It felt strange to be interacting with people again and seeing how up and down my moods could go in response to someone else. It felt like too much at times and it was tempting to curl up in a ball and be left alone, but then I would miss seeing this cute face looking up at me that was now only mildly pink.

"You're blushing."

"Of course I am! That was embarrassing!"

"But you wanted me to see it? Why?"

"I don't know," Alicia shrugged, "I guess I wanted you to know I'm attracted to you?"

"Well, I was starting to get that feeling because you want to spend time with me. I don't have to post it on Facebook for you to know I'm attracted to you, do I?"

"No," she said and looked down, so I put my hand under her chin and made her look at me. "I really do think you're pretty." I wanted to kiss her so bad right then, but we were on the sidewalk so I took her hand and started walking. She was very pink and it was starting to crack me up that I had the advantage of olive skin. I never thought about it like that before, but Alicia had an extra indicator of her emotions that I didn't have to deal with. I was smiling to myself and Alicia asked, "What's so funny?"

"Nothing. I just think it's cute how you blush."

"Damn you, Ray, for making me blush." But she was smiling so I knew she didn't mind.

As we got close to the SummerStage, I could see that it was already really crowded. The theater seating was full and people were putting blankets down on the surrounding grass area to hear the music. We decided to do the same and Alicia took her little blanket out of her bag. I looked around and said, "Wow, there are a lot of broke people in New York looking for some free entertainment."

Alicia laughed and said, "Who says they're broke? There are just a lot of people in New York! Besides, this is way better than sitting in a dark movie theater on a beautiful summer day."

"Yes, way better."

"I'm on a pretty strict budget myself, you know. I only work thirty hours a week."

"Really?"

"Yeah, since I go to school. My parents help me out a

little bit."

"And your company is cool with you working part time?"

"Yes because they think I am going to work for them when I get my CPA."

"Are you?"

"Well, yes, for a few years maybe. Eventually I want to be self-employed."

Just then a guy came onto the stage and introduced the band. I started thinking about how Alicia had her life planned and goals set and I had just been surviving with no plan. I really couldn't understand what she might see in me. The band came on and this black guy was playing some crazy piano, all classical and fast, then he slowed down and started just playing two irritating notes over and over, but singing and talking about New Orleans over the music.

"Hey, did you catch their name?" I asked Alicia, right as a sax, trombone and drums joined in, but she couldn't hear me. She was smiling with big eyes and looked excited by the music, or maybe just the atmosphere. I knew the guys had talent, although it was kind of jazzy and not my taste, but I loved being outside sitting next to Alicia and listening to music surrounded by all the people. Some people got up and started dancing, which was completely crazy. I'm a pretty decent dancer, but this music had an unpredictable beat and wasn't very danceable, so the dancers were pretty brave or stupid or maybe a bit intoxicated – I couldn't tell. I felt kind of embarrassed for them and hoped they would sit down, but after a while I just appreciated the city vibe of the whole thing. The energy was contagious, like just being a part of the music.

The song went on for a very long time. They seemed to be improvising, each of the musicians taking their turn and when it finally stopped they got great applause and I asked again, "Who are they?" Alicia took a flyer out of her bag that had a SummerStage calendar on it and it said, "John Batiste & Stay Human." I thought to myself, *Now there is a good goal for me. I'm gonna stay human, I'm gonna stay among the humans.*

After a few songs that all sounded pretty similar, Alicia asked if I wanted to move away and I said sure. We walked about a hundred yards over to a tree and put the blanket back down. We could still hear the music, but she said she wanted to be able to talk to me and I agreed. We talked about music and both agreed that what we were hearing wasn't our taste, but it was one of the cool things about New York, seeing and hearing music performed live like that on a Sunday afternoon.

Alicia opened her bag and I saw that she had brought more strawberries and another sandwich. She gave it all to me saying she felt a little too queasy to eat, but she accepted my apple. She still felt a little sick and really tired and I told her she should lie down, that we didn't need to go anywhere. I was leaning against the tree and she put her head in my lap and I got to play with her soft pretty hair. I felt like I was in heaven with the music in the background, the sun shining, sitting in the shade with Alicia's head in my lap. She was just lying there with her eyes closed, and it really gave me a chance to study her.

I like how Alicia is curvy. Her dress was blue and she was wearing those sandals that have a strap between the first two toes. Her toenails were painted red and they looked like perfect little rounded rectangles, all lined up like bricks, each one a little bigger than the next and the fifth one being much larger. I was thinking about how Carlos had a thing for feet and used to say, "You can tell a lot about a girl by how she keeps her feet." I never took him all that seriously, but one time we were at a party and I hooked up with this girl and I was trying to get Carlos to hook up with her friend. It was something we often did for each other, but this time

Carlos was, "Hell no, man," and I argued the she was cute but Carlos said, "Check out the dogs on that dog, bro!" and he actually shuddered. I thought he was just being picky but I did look at her feet and said, "Aw, man. Never mind." She really did have ugly feet with chipped nail polish and cracked heels and even had hair on her toes, and I got it. I don't know why that girl didn't just wear some shoes that covered her feet, but I got it and said, "Okay, man, it's cool." We didn't hook up and went out drinking more instead. I was laughing about this to myself when Alicia asked, "What's so funny?"

"Aw, nothing. I was just thinking my friend Carlos would like you, that's all."

"Will I get to meet him?"

"Good question. Maybe he'll come visit."

"How come you don't go home and visit?"

"Oh, I will eventually. It's just that my brother and dad have always been really close and I was close with my mom and now we don't seem like a family as much. Feels like a car with three wheels. Plus, my dad let the house get all sick and gross and he even made my old room into an office."

"Well, that's better than my parents, who kept my room exactly like it was. An 'Alicia Museum.' It's like they don't think I can make it and they are ready for me to fail at any moment and move back home." Alicia shifted onto her side and turned her head and closed her eyes again and her face was dangerously close to my crotch. I tried keeping my cool about it, but it was way too arousing having this pretty girl with her face right in my lap. I started doing math problems in my head so I wouldn't get busted with a hard on.

"I should probably get going soon, Ray," she said after I

71

had divided seven hundred twenty two by three. Of course she had to study again. She wasn't kidding about studying all the time, but I wasn't going to show my disappointment. I was glad to get to spend a few hours with her and now I could walk her home.

We talked about the upcoming week and I wanted to take her somewhere that would be very Manhattan but not too expensive, then I got an idea. "Hey, have you ever been to the Carnegie Deli?"

"No! But I've always wanted to go there! That is like a total icon of New York and I've wanted to go there for months!" She answered in a very animated way.

"Well, what day are you free? You can get off the subway at the 57th Street station and I'll meet you there."

"I don't have to meet with my study group on Wednesday!" She seemed genuinely excited and I was happy about that.

"Perfect. But I'll still try to meet you at the subway tomorrow, if you don't mind."

"I'd love that." Her face was beaming and I felt like my chest was swelling because my heart was growing. It made me smile back at her and we were now standing on her stairs smiling at each other until she got self-conscious and looked away. Even though it was still daylight, I wanted to kiss her right there on the stoop.

She was on the step above me with her hands on my shoulders as mine were on her hips. I pulled her whole body close to me and kissed her lips, gently at first, then hungrily as she responded to my kiss. I finally let myself kiss her the way I'd wanted to since the day I met her. Full body contact, gently parting her lips with my tongue, gently dipping in and making contact with hers as she responded in kind. I felt her hand move to the back of my neck as we alternated between gentle and deeper kisses. I could have kissed her like that forever, but some jerk came down the stairs and muttered the cliché, "Get a room." Alicia just laughed and came in for one more kiss. I really liked kissing her.

"Bye, Ray. I'll see you tomorrow," she walked up the stoop and turned and waved before going through the door.

On Monday I showed up at the penthouse to work on the kitchen remodel. The new cabinets had arrived and Lenny was teaching me how to install them. Mostly he showed me what he was doing while I held things in place or handed things to him since these were extremely expensive cabinets.

Don made a trip down to the truck and when he came back he said, "Hey, Lenny, check out Ray. Notice he's wearing work boots now?"

I explained, "I noticed you and Lenny wear them, so I figured I should too."

"Hear that, Lenny? He noticed we were wearin' 'em. You notice we got our own tools, eh, Ray?"

"Yeah, I noticed that too."

Lenny said in a hushed voice, "Don't let him bust your balls, Ray. I know for a fact he ain't paying you enough for you to start buyin' tools."

"I heard that, Lenny. Don't worry, I was just thinking about offering Ray more money. Don't go talking a bunch a shit and starting up a mutiny."

"I'll take it," I said.

"Take what?" Don asked.

"Your offer. More money. I'll take it."

Don laughed and said, "I ain't even made an offer yet. Ain't you gonna negotiate?"

"No," I answered, "I like working with you guys and anything more is better than what I'm getting now."

Don laughed and said, "You hear that, Lenny? The kid likes workin' with us. Kid, you are something else. You gotta learn not to be so trusting or you're gonna get taken advantage of."

I thought about what he said; it was just like something my dad would say and it was true in some cases. Sometimes I trusted the wrong people like Thomas and Jeff, but I didn't think Don was like that. He had been more than fair to me so far.

It took all day, but we finished the kitchen and it came out amazing, like something out of a magazine. I took some photos of it with my phone and sent them to my dad. Don told me he wanted to talk to me for a minute while Lenny was outside and that is when he offered me a new pay rate and told me I would have to go on payroll and start getting taxes taken out. I thanked him but asked if I could still get paid cash this week because I had a few bills to catch up on and he said, "Good negotiating, Ray."

Then he gave me a used motorized drill and told me I needed to keep track of it and keep it charged up. He told me to put my initials on it because sometimes they disappear from the jobsite. Since I walk or take the subway, he offered to keep it in the locked tool box on the truck, but I told him I wanted to take it home and practice drilling holes.

"What? You want to practice drilling?"

"Yeah," I answered, "I wanna get fast like Lenny." I

noticed Lenny could put in about five screws in the time it took me to do one and I wanted to practice. Lenny was walking up to us and Don said, "You hear that, Lenny? The kid wants to take his drill home and practice. Good lord almighty, where the hell did this kid come from!"

Lenny smacked me on the back and said, "Ray, it'll take you two decades to get as good as me and by then I'll be retired." Both guys were laughing but I didn't mind. It was the best workday ever, and I still had time to make it to Alicia's subway if I put my drill in the backpack and ran.

Alicia looked upset. Her face was all puffy which made me think she had been crying, but her eyes were normal. Her expression was different though. She walked up and gave me a hug and I backed her up and held her shoulders and asked, "What's wrong?"

"I got a B on my test."

"Oh, is that all? You had me worried for a second."

"Is that all?! Ray, you don't understand! I studied really hard for that test. Now I have to earn a 95% on my next test to keep my A in the class! Do you know how hard that will be?"

"No, I don't, really. What would happen if you got a B?"

"I don't get B's!" she snapped.

I couldn't believe how upset she was. She started to turn and walk so I walked alongside her. I wanted to tell her I got a raise and my own drill, but it didn't seem like the right time. No B's. That was intense. She was right: I didn't understand, but I could tell she was really bothered.

"I feel like Sisyphus, pushing that heavy, huge rock up the hill. I work so hard, Ray." She sounded like a sad little girl, like she might cry.

"I know you do, Alicia." I didn't know what else to say, so I figured I'd better just agree with her. She was quiet now, and I was hoping she wasn't thinking I distracted her too much from her studying. I took her hand and she let me. It was a long quiet walk through a noisy city.

When we got to her place, she said, "Thanks for not taking my bad mood personally. Seeing you was the best part of my day. I was really glad to see you at the station."

I lifted her hand to my mouth and kissed it. The back side was covered in scratches and some of them had scabbed over, so I asked, "What happened to your hand?"

"I don't know." She pulled her hand away. "Don't forget we have a date on Wednesday," she said, changing the subject.

"How could I forget?" I laughed. Then she apologized that she had to go study and of course I didn't want her to feel bad about that, and I almost made a joke about having homework myself, but drilling holes would sound pretty stupid compared to accounting so I just said I had stuff to do too and kissed her goodbye.

It was a quick kiss and I watched her walk inside, feeling kind of sorry for her that she felt that much pressure to get A's. I never put that kind of pressure on myself. She was right. I didn't understand. It seemed like soon she would realize I'm a slacker and get sick of me. Well, at least I am a well-read slacker. Time to go see my man William.

My favorite thing about the Mid-Manhattan Library is the ceiling. As I was stood waiting for William to quit talking to two middle-aged women, I passed the time staring at the ornate ceiling with painted clouds. I didn't notice he was free until he said, "Tell me, Ray, how did I fare? Were the books to your liking?"

"*Let the Great World Spin* was great. I'm still reading *Adventures of Cavalier and Clay.*"

"Did you have a favorite story in the collection?"

"Yeah, probably the one about the preacher, but they were all good. I don't usually go for short stories, but the way they were all tied together was really cool."

William rubbed his chin as if he had a beard, but he was clean shaven and very well groomed. He raised one eyebrow at me. I wish I could do that. It made him look very intellectual. "Are you prepared to enjoy another Manhattan adventure?"

"Not yet, since I still have the other one, plus I picked up some used books. I actually came looking for something else," I said.

"And what, pray tell, might that be?"

"Maslow. And Sisyphus. I remember learning about Sisyphus but can't remember the story and I want to know what they are about."

"Well, Ray, choosing literature is my forte, but please satisfy my curiosity and tell me what sparked your interest in Psychology and Greek Mythology?"

"A girl," I admitted and William laughed, knowingly. I went on, "I never went to college but I'm seeing this girl and.... I just don't want to seem ignorant. Can you give me some advice on some stuff I should read? Things that most people would know if they went to college?"

William laughed and said, "I respect the hedonic nature of your motivation. I respond well to hedonic motivation myself. Listen, Ray, I am going to print out a synopsis explaining the contributions of both Maslow and Sisyphus. Then I am going to give you a calendar which shows educational events conducted here at the library and circle those I consider worthwhile."

"Cool. My girl is usually busy studying at night and I don't have a TV, so that would be good."

"Ray, did I just hear you say you don't own a television? It attests to my staunch heterosexual nature that I did not kiss you just now."

"Whoa! Down, boy! I'm no intellectual. Just broke."

Just then two women walked by and whispered, "Hi, William!" in unison. He nodded towards them and said, "Ladies." Right behind them was a woman dressed in black with thigh-high boots. She looked like Laura Croft and I couldn't take my eyes off her, but she didn't even notice me. She kept her eyes fixed on William and she said, "Help me find a book, William," in a sultry voice.

"Yes, ma'am," he answered and handed me a few sheets of paper, which I knew was my cue to leave. I felt my phone buzzing anyway and said, "See ya later, man."

It was a text from Alicia that said, "Goodnight, Ray. Try not to think about me too much."

I texted her back, "I got an F on that assignment."

6 - PASTRAMI

I watched Alicia get off the subway and almost didn't recognize her at first. I was expecting to see her in her professional clothing, but she had on dark jeans, brown boots that stopped just below the knee, and an orange top that was shaped like a triangle and hung off one shoulder.

"Damn, girl. You look hot!" I whispered, as I hugged her and gave her a quick kiss. Then I pushed her back to arm's length to get another look at her. She smiled and said, "I changed clothes after work."

"I would have guessed so. That is not a very professional ensemble. It would have been too distracting for your male coworkers." I had stopped by my apartment and changed out of my work boots and put on the only button-up shirt I own. Carnegie's is super casual, but I still wanted to look good for her and now I was really glad that I made the effort.

She took my hand and we started walking through the station when I heard, "Ray, Ray, Ray!" I turned toward the sound and saw Robbie looking pretty grungy, as usual. "Ray, my man!" He stuck out his hand and I shook it as he patted me on the shoulder with the other one. "Look at you, man! All cleaned up! On a date too?" He looked Alicia up and down savoring her with his bugged-out eyes. "Mmm, mmm, mmm, look at you."

"Hey Robbie, this is Alicia."

Alicia said "Hi" and did not stick out her hand. I guess Robbie looked a little intimidating. I felt nervous that he might say something revealing and tried to keep the conversation short.

"Wait a minute," he looked back at me. "Is this the girl from the subway?"

"Yeah, this is her."

"Damn, man! I knew it!" He turned to Alicia and said, "I was there! I was there the day you hugged Ray and rocked his world. I saw the whole damn thing. I was there another time too!"

"You were?" Alicia asked, head tilted to one side like she was trying to remember.

"Yeah, well, Ray told me to stay quiet, that's why you didn't notice me," Robbie turned to me to wink, probably reminding me that he did me a favor – one I paid him for. "Speaking of which, . . Hey, Ray, you got three dollars on you? I'm a little short for my subway pass. I'll get you back next time I see you." Robbie was scratching himself the whole time he was talking.

"Sure," I said and handed Robbie a five. He didn't offer change and I didn't care; I just wanted to get away before he said too much. I could feel myself starting to sweat.

"Thanks, man. You lookin' good by the way. Good to see you all cleaned up. And you," he turned to Alicia. "Lookin' fine as always!"

"Thanks," Alicia smiled politely.

Robbie left us and I sighed in relief. "That was kinda weird. How do you know him?" Alicia asked.

"Just from the stations," I admitted truthfully. "You meet some very interesting people in subway stations." I squeezed her hand, wanting to steer the conversation away from why I am on such friendly terms with a mildly crazy, severely homeless guy.

"Yes, I've met someone pretty interesting in a subway station," Alicia squeezed my hand back as we walked out of the station and up to the fresh air on the bustling sidewalk.

My rent was paid and I had eighty five dollars left over, thanks to Don paying me extra for working late the previous day. I wasn't that worried about running out of money now that I had a consistent job and was put on payroll. I reported on my unemployment form that I had a new job, so that would be cut off, but I was about to run out of unemployment benefits anyway. I had a new feeling of security, not complete security, but more than I had felt in many months. It made me think of Maslow's pyramid and I didn't want to get cocky, but it felt like I was moving up. I was even allowing myself to have hope about Alicia. I felt much more comfortable around her and wasn't plagued by the thought that every time I saw her would be the last. And I actually was able to take her on a date.

When we arrived at Carnegie's there was a line outside, but that didn't concern me at all. If anything, it gave me more time to talk to Alicia. I could smell smoked meat and my stomach was rumbling and I hoped she didn't hear it. She asked if I minded if she took a photo and of course I didn't. She said she didn't want to embarrass me by looking like a tourist and I honestly said she couldn't embarrass me if she tried. Obviously she doesn't know the humiliation of reaching into a trashcan looking for food; taking a cellphone pic was nothing to be embarrassed about.

Alicia chattered on and on about Carnegie's. Apparently she had done some research online and knew the history of the place, "The food is supposed to be great, but some people complain about the service and there were many complaints about the share charge."

"What's that?"

"They charge you $ 3.00 if you share your food with someone."

"That seems weird. So you have to order your own sandwich and just throw food away when there are so many people hungry in this city?" I complained.

"Yes, that's true. I didn't think about that. I just wonder why they make their sandwiches so ginormous? No one can eat the whole thing anyway."

"I can," I stated confidently.

"Have you seen them?" she asked.

"Oh yeah, I've eaten one before." Alicia got a funny look on her face, so I teased her, "I bring all my dates here. It's kind of a test, if they can't eat the whole sandwich, I don't go out with them again."

Alicia got a panicked look on her face, and I saw instantly that I'd better not mess with her too much. "I'm joking. I ate here once with Carlos and we challenged each other to eat the whole thing. We both finished our sandwiches, but we were hurtin' afterwards."

Alicia laughed and said, "Impressive. Do you think you

can do it again?"

"I sure do. I skipped lunch."

Alicia giggled and asked, "Do you mind if I check us in on Facebook?"

"Why would I mind?"

"I don't know. In case there's some girl you don't want to know that you're out on a date."

I laughed at that, but then it occurred to me that maybe she kept posting on Facebook because she had a guy back in California, maybe she was trying to make someone jealous. "What about you?"

"Oh, there might be a few guys who are going to be disappointed, but I don't want them to think I'm available. I know it probably seems pretty immature that I post on Facebook so much, but I want my friends and family to know that I am doing okay and that I am out having fun, not just working and going to school all the time. Some of my friends are really interested in what it's like here, and I get pretty excited talking about it." Alicia was going on and on about how she loved New York and how different it was, but I was not being a good listener. My mind was still stuck on the statement that she didn't want other guys to think she was available. She wanted people to know she was with me. My mood was skyrocketing and she was still yapping about New York, so I pulled her in close and kissed her.

"Wow, what was that for?" Alicia was smiling.

"I don't know, I just felt like kissing you."

Alicia was beaming up at me and said, "Well if I kissed you every time I felt like it, I wouldn't even be able to hold down a job or go to school. I'd end up homeless and wandering the streets."

This made me laugh and stung me at the same time. "Alicia, do you think that's what causes people to be homeless?" I whispered in her ear, "All these men and women just kissed too much and didn't show up to work?"

Alicia laughed, "No, but that sounds like a lot more fun than being a drug addict or alcoholic."

"It sure does, but not all homeless people are drug addicts or alcoholics, you know."

"Oh, very true! Some are mentally ill, some are down on their luck. I think it is a multi-faceted problem..."

I was trying to listen to this serious discussion, but I found myself totally distracted by Alicia's exposed shoulder and thinking about kissing it. I wondered if she could be wearing a bra because no strap was visible. I looked down at her tits and it seemed like she was. Luckily, we got a table right at that moment, before I got caught staring at her chest.

"Wow, Ray! They weren't kidding about the size of those sandwiches!" She whispered exuberantly. We were led to our table and a waiter set down menus without saying anything. "There's no way you can eat that whole thing!"

"That sounds like a dare. A pretty easy one too."

The waiter came back and set a dish of pickles on our table and still didn't say anything. I immediately tasted one and was blown away by that sour crunchy flavor. I wasn't sure if they were extraordinary or if I was extremely hungry, or if the fact they were free made them even more delicious. Alicia was studying the menu and said, "I don't know why I'm even looking, I already checked out the menu online and know exactly what I am having."

"A pastrami sandwich, right?" I guessed.

"No, the Greek salad."

"Alicia! You cannot come to Carnegie's and order a salad! You have to have a sandwich!"

Alicia expression changed to worry as she leaned in and whispered, "Please Ray, don't make me eat a sandwich."

Her face was killing me right then – she looked so young and vulnerable. Of course I answered with, "I was teasing you, Alicia. Eat anything you want. I don't care."

Relief washed over her face, right as the waiter came. Alicia ordered a Greek salad and a diet Coke; I ordered a Pastrami sandwich and a beer. I was really looking forward to tasting the first beer I'd had in a long time. "You'll try a bite of my sandwich, though, won't you?"

"Is it pork?"

I laughed at that, "It's kosher."

"Oh yeah, I forgot," she laughed. "Sorry to be such a pain in the ass."

"You're not a pain in the ass. Why would you even say that?"

Alicia shrugged and picked up a pickle. The waiter came back with our drinks and said he forgot to ask for my ID, so I took out my wallet and showed him, and then left my wallet on the table. "What's that?" Alicia gestured toward my wallet.

"My wallet?"

"No, that piece of paper sticking out."

"Oh, that's the note you gave me." I pulled it out and showed her. It was the note that said her name and that hugging me was the bright spot of her day. I like to take it out and look at it every once in a while.

Alicia cheeks were turning bright red, "I can't believe you saved that in your wallet. That is so sweet but so embarrassing."

"Why?"

"I gave you a note. That is so... I don't know... high school."

"I never thought that. I was glad you did."

Just then our food came and my sandwich was about eight inches tall. I made the Sign of the Cross as a joke, like I was going to need help eating it and Alicia asked, "Are you Catholic?"

"Not practicing, although I did go to church the other day. They were having a rummage sale and I got this shirt." I couldn't believe I said that and instantly regretted it.

"Oh cool! I like that shirt! Next time they have a rummage sale, will you take me?"

"You like rummage sales?" I asked, genuinely surprised and relieved.

"Yes, I like a lot of things," she answered.

"You don't like pork."

Alicia laughed, "True, I don't eat pork. But I do like guys who have green eyes and can devour really big sandwiches."

"Well, I'm about to be your hero." I said, and dug in.

After we finished eating, I asked Alicia if she wanted to

take the subway together back to her regular station and she asked if we could walk.

"Really? It's kind of far. But I would like to walk off this sandwich." I said, rubbing my abdomen.

"What about cutting through the park? Is it safe? Have you been in the park at night?"

"Oh yeah, I've spent a lot of time in the park at night. You technically aren't supposed to be there after 1:00 a.m., but at this time of night the upper part is safe. There's even a bunch of joggers at night and people out walking dogs after work. But I wouldn't want to think of you walking there alone after dark. Are you okay to walk in those boots?"

"Oh yeah, they're really comfortable." Alicia answered. "Thanks for being considerate, though."

"I used to go out with this girl who would wear really high heels and she always ended up mad because her feet hurt. Sometimes we would have to park the car and walk a block to the club or a restaurant and she would get so pissed. I liked the way the shoes looked, but every time she wore heels I knew we were going to get in a fight. I liked her better in her sneakers," I laughed.

"Was that in New York or before you moved here?"

"Oh, that was back at home. I haven't had a car or a girlfriend since coming to New York."

"Well, you don't need a car," Alicia laughed. "That is one thing I don't miss about California."

"Yeah? What do you miss about California?"

"Aside from my friends, the weather," Alicia whispered,

like it was something she didn't want to admit, even though no one was around or interested. "It is just so easy. I appreciate the change of seasons and all, but in California it didn't even snow where I lived."

"Never?"

"Never. I would have to drive about an hour to get to snow and mountains. Big mountains, Ray, not hills, although we have rolling hills too. The topography is so diverse, I could drive five minutes and be at the beach, or two hours and be in the desert, or three hours and be in the central valley where there are miles and miles of farmland."

"I never associate California with farms."

"Oh, you'd be surprised. We used to drive to see my grandma and for five hours straight we sat in the car seeing nothing but farms, orchards mostly. Do you know what they were growing?"

"Oranges?"

"Good guess, but no. Almonds. California's main crop is almonds and they grow almost all the almonds consumed in the world, with Spain being a very distant second. I looked it up online while we were driving through miles and miles of short trees."

"Are you sure you don't want to be a teacher?" I laughed and Alicia laughed too. "I've noticed you like to research things."

"That's true. I am very curious. And I noticed you like to read a lot."

"Yes, I do. How about you? Do you read much fiction?"

"I used to, but with all my studying I haven't been able to indulge in a novel for a long time. I always feel like I need to study, even on the subway. Plus, my mind is really full, but I loved to read growing up."

We had walked into the park and I took a big whiff and told Alicia to smell it. The park smells different at night. Instead of just grass, there are other plant smells that become prominent, things I can never smell during the daytime. I stopped Alicia and told her to look around. We stood there turning a slow circle admiring the skyline. It does look so very different at night, very beautiful. It is an odd feeling to see so many lights on, knowing there are so many people close by, yet we were almost alone.

"Look how pretty the Essex House looks at night!" Alicia said in her excited-girl way.

"Look how pretty Alicia Klaer looks at night," I said, looking down at her. I was looking at her sweet and effervescent face, marveling at how pretty she looked under the starlight. I bent down like I was about to kiss her, but then made a sharp right turn and kissed that bare shoulder I had been staring at all night. Alicia gasped and I stopped and looked at her and she giggled and said, "I thought you were about to kiss me."

"I was. And I still am. I just wanted to start with this shoulder I've been admiring all night."

I went back to that shoulder and kissed it again, slowly, but this time I didn't stop. I kissed that bare shoulder and gradually worked my way up her neck, travelling from the collarbone up to the spot below her ear, meandering, tasting her skin along the way, inhaling the smell of her hair. I slowly kissed my way across her jawline all the way to her mouth and by this time I noticed she was breathless. I was pleasantly surprised by how eagerly she was responding to my kisses. She was pressed up against me and I wasn't even pulling her in. As we continued exploring each other's mouth, I allowed my hands to do a little exploring down south to that delicious ass I had admired so many times.

I heard the steps of a jogger coming up and broke the kiss and looked down at Alicia's grinning face. We started walking again, silently. There were plenty of people running and walking through the park and we passed a few homeless people sleeping on benches.

"That's so sad," Alicia said when we passed a guy on a bench who had covered himself in cardboard.

"Not that sad," I answered. "It's pretty warm out. The winter is when it's really sad."

When we got to Alicia's apartment, she stopped on the steps and turned around to face me.

"Ray, I want to ask you something, but I don't want you to take it the wrong way."

"What is it?" I asked, suddenly a little nervous.

"Well, you know I need to go in and I have to wake up early tomorrow, but I was wondering if Friday you might want to come over and I'll cook dinner for you and maybe we can watch a movie, but... well... I just don't want you to think, I mean, I really like you, obviously, but I don't want to give the impression..." Alicia sighed and went on, "Some guys would think it means... and it's not that...."

I was getting amused by Alicia's stammering and I knew exactly what she was trying to say so I decided to let her off the hook. In fact, my confidence around her was to a point now that I felt I could use my "Sha-Nay-Nay" voice on her. That is what Carlos called it when I used my "strong black woman" voice and it always cracked him up, so I said, "Alicia, I will come to your apartment and eat with you, but I am NOT having sex with you, so just get that idea out of your head!" I waved my finger in a "no" fashion.

Alicia started laughing and put her hand over her mouth, so I went on, rubbing my chest with one hand, "Cuz my body is a temple, and I respect myself, and you're gonna have to respect me too, so don't think just cuz you cook dinner that gives you free access to my boxer-briefs!" I put my hand on my hip.

Alicia was really cracking up now. "I am not that easy, mmm, mmm. I'll put a padlock on my belt buckle so you know, these pants are staying on! And just like Cinderella, I'm leaving before midnight, so don't even try to seduce me. Girl, you are just going to have to try and control yourself and be patient." I was jutting my hips back and forth now to accentuate my point.

"Oh my god, Ray, you are so funny."

"I'm serious, though, Alicia," I said in my normal voice. "I'm not the kind of guy who thinks that dinner means sex. I'm in no hurry."

"Thank you," she said, smiling at me and pulling me in for a hug. I kissed her goodbye and said, "But please cover up those shoulders. I'm only human."

Thursday morning I was awakened by my own raging hard-on. Apparently my dick got the message that we now had privacy and demanded to be heard on a daily basis. I guess good ole Maslow considered this a "physiological" need, so I didn't trip on it at all, but I was still very careful not to imagine Alicia, which was difficult after that kissing in the park.

Carlos and I have this expression, "False Advertisers."

That is what we call girls who put all this effort into dressing in a really sexy way to attract guys, but aren't really into sex at all. The way Alicia kissed me back was extremely passionate and sexy, yet she didn't need to wear a mini skirt or show off her cleavage. Although I was curious about her cleavage. Very curious.

I did some crunches and sets of push ups after I got up off the couch. I don't have any fat on my body and have a tendency to get too skinny and now I had to consider being seen without a shirt. There were all kinds of things on my mind now that I wasn't using all that energy worrying about staying warm or fed. I laughed at myself thinking it was like a second puberty I was having. I hoped I didn't get any zits.

When I got to the address Don had texted me, Lenny was there but Don wasn't. "This is going to be a quick one," Lenny said. "This lady barely lived here and kept it real clean, so we just need to do some touch up paint and get rid of the stuff she left behind."

The apartment did look really clean with just a few nail holes where pictures were hung and a futon and dining table left behind. "Why'd she leave this furniture? It looks new."

"Who knows? Probably didn't want to hassle with it. I'm going to take the dining table. Do you want the futon?"

"Are you serious? That's way better than what I have now. But I can't get it home."

"I'll drop you off and we can take it in the truck," Lenny offered. "I can't see us workin' past noon today, but Don is off lookin' at a big job. If he gets it, we are gonna be busy as hell. Probably gonna have to hire some help and work Saturdays."

I thought about soccer, but it was a fleeting thought. I could give up soccer for a while if it meant getting on my feet financially, especially considering I no longer had roommates to help with the rent. Lenny was right, we were done by noon and today's work was so light he talked a lot and told me about his kids. I liked how Lenny was when he was by himself. He worked hard and was quiet most of the time, but he was really easygoing and I get along with those kinds of guys really well. They seem rare, almost an endangered species, especially in the construction world.

When we finished the apartment, we loaded the table and futon into the truck and made the short drive over to my place, which took plenty of time because of the traffic. I started to feel anxious about Lenny seeing my place. We double parked with the emergency flashers on, so at least I knew it would be all business and over quickly. When I opened the door, he didn't react at all, except to say we could take the couch and cot out and he would drop them off at the dump. I was really feeling indebted to him for helping me. With the couch and cot gone, my place seemed, well… not big, but normal-sized by New York standards. At least it was clean. Lenny finally looked around and said, "You should paint that one wall a different color. That would really help. Let's go see what we have in the truck."

We walked down to the truck that was now loaded down with furniture; he couldn't get to the paint cans, but he did pull out some sandpaper. "Tomorrow, see what we got in here. I think there is some of that mocha paint left over. That'll look good with that red futon. Meanwhile, get the wall ready and sand your coffee table. We've got some stain and polyurethane you can put on it." I thanked him and shook his hand. I walked back upstairs thinking about how different Don and Lenny were from my dad. With plumbing, it was all about getting things to work. With Don and Lenny, they cared about how things looked and I do too. I realized that is why I liked this type of work better, even better than the job I had with Carlos doing maintenance.

I started sanding the coffee table while I waited until it was time to meet Alicia at the station, but around four o'clock I got a text from her saying she was sick and didn't go to work that day. My first concern was that she would cancel our date tomorrow, but I caught myself feeling selfish. My second thought was that I had known her only a short time and she already was sick once before. That seemed kind of weird; she didn't look unhealthy, but maybe it was just a coincidence. I decided to give her a call.

"Hi, Ray!" She sounded happy but her voice was scratchy.

"Are you okay?"

"Oh yeah, it's just my stomach bothers me sometimes. I'll be okay by tomorrow for sure."

I sighed in relief but wondered how she could be certain? Maybe she just had female issues, so I didn't question it. We ended up talking on the phone for an hour. I learned that her longest relationship was two years and that she was still friendly with the guy and he was even dating one of her friends and she was okay with it. She said she started dating a guy she met in New York, but he complained that she was too busy. I told her about my old girlfriends. There had been two significant relationships but nothing serious since I moved.

Alicia told me that she feels a lot of prejudice because she is from California. That never occurred to me, but she said they tease her at work sometimes, saying she is from "La-la land."

"Well, you guys did elect 'The Terminator' for Governor," I said.

"Point taken," she agreed. "But there is this attitude I pick up on that I wasn't properly educated because I didn't attend Ivy League schools."

"Yeah, I don't get that at my work," I laughed. I told here

how we might be getting really busy and I might have to work Saturdays. Alicia said that was good because I couldn't complain about her being busy and I told her I wasn't going to complain about that anyway.

She finally said she had better go and study and we said goodnight until tomorrow. Alicia said not to worry about the subway, but come over at seven and she hoped I wasn't a picky eater.

That made me laugh and I said, "No, I am definitely not a picky eater."

After we said goodbye and hung up, I took a hot shower, something I don't think I'll ever take for granted again. All night I reveled in the thought that I was going to Alicia's apartment the next day. A date with Subway Girl, Alicia. I fell asleep on my new futon with a book about an adventure in New York on my chest and a grin on my face.

7 – STIR FRY

Friday I got home from work and still had a few hours to kill before going to Alicia's, so I decided to call my dad. He answered the phone, but I was immediately reminded why I usually call him on Sunday mornings. It was obvious he had been drinking, but he wasn't slurring, just being talkative. I told him I was still working, and then I told him I'd met a girl.

"Yeah, I figured that," he said. I could hear ice clinking in the background like he was swirling his drink. "I noticed your cell phone usage just went through the roof."

"Oh, sorry, Dad. Do you want me to send some money to cover it?"

"Nah, don't worry about it. I got one of those mega-plans since it's a business expense. Just don't be going on the internet too much lookin' at porn. Your brother showed me how you can watch porn right there on the damn phone. The tiny screen is too small for my eyes, but not your brother. You gotta be careful with that shit, Raymond, you can get over-stimulated and then the normal stuff doesn't work for ya anymore and you start gettin' weird. I tell ya back in my day we thought seein' a set a hooters was a big deal. One of the kids in the neighborhood would get his hands on a Playboy and it was a big deal! We'd pass it around and I'd stare at those babes for hours, ya know what I mean? Now, one or two clicks and the things you can see! Hell, your brother – he showed me one…"….

I zoned out after that. Here's the thing about my dad: he always dominates the conversation. I wanted to tell him about Alicia and how smart and pretty she is, but instead he starts talking to me about porn and I'm really not interested. As soon as he paused to take a drink I tried to tell him I had a date and couldn't talk much longer, but as soon as I mentioned I was going to her house he launched into his spiel about condoms, "Cuz I got lucky with your mom, she was a keeper, but most of the time guys get stuck and regret it. Hell, not to mention all the diseases. Raymond, you dunno know where this girl's been, you could be number two or three for her just this week for all you know. Hell, remember your friend…"

"Dad, I'm sorry I have to cut you off, but someone's at the door," I lied before I got really pissed. I hung up the phone and saw that it was 6:10 p.m., still plenty of time to walk to Alicia's apartment. I could take the subway, but I like walking and I wanted to pick up some flowers on the way.

At the flower shop I stood in front of the display of bouquets wondering what to get. I couldn't spend too much money, but nothing seemed quite right. The arrangements on display looked kind of audacious. I didn't want to buy a single rose because that seemed kind of cliché and I had heard that different colors mean different things and I wasn't sure what they meant.

I'd hate to give her the "Sorry someone died" color by mistake.

There was a girl working there, but she didn't look anxious to help. She had her nose buried in a book in the typical anti-social fashion, uneager to help me. She was perched on a stool and had huge black-framed glasses. She had that cool nerdy look going on with black hair in a sharp angled cut and colorful tattoos covering one arm. She was very pretty, but not in the soft-pretty way like Alicia. This girl was all sharp edges and color, like a piece of modern art.

There were flowers sold individually in buckets and I was considering putting a few together in a do-it-yourself bouquet, but I wasn't sure if that was allowed or what to do. I walked up to the girl at the counter and noticed the book she was reading was called *The Buffalo Hunter*.

"Is that a western?" I asked.

"What?" She looked up from her book, then turned it over and looked at the cover. Laughing she said, "No, it isn't. It actually takes place in New York."

"Really? What's it about?"

"This lonely creepy guy who reads a lot. He gets so into the books he is reading that he actually loses touch with reality."

"Oh, I didn't realize my biography was out yet," I joked and got a laugh out of Flower Girl.

"You can't be that lonely if you are in here buying flowers for a girl."

"How do you know that? I could be buying flower for my mom or something."

"No, you aren't. I've been at this awhile and when guys

come in to buy flowers there are three types. The first type is the 'I-fucked-up-sorry' guy. They're so guilty I can usually make good money off them. Then we have the, 'It's-her-birthday-or-anniversary-and-I have-no-imagination' guy. And then there is the least common type who is newly dating someone. They stress out the most."

"Yeah, what about the 'I-have-only-fifteen-dollars-but-don't-want-to-look-cheap' guy?"

"Oooh, a double stressor. I feel sorry for you!" She laughed at me and I didn't think it was funny, but she finally offered to help me. "What is she like? Give me five adjectives."

After pausing for a few seconds to come up with an authentic list, I answered, "Cheerful, enthusiastic, smart, sweet, hot."

"Gerber daisies," she stated, confidently.

"Aren't daises known for being cheap?"

"Not Gerbers. Come have a look."

They looked so perfect they almost looked like fake flowers. When I saw the vibrant orange Gerbers, they reminded me of Alicia's sexy shoulder shirt and her happy face. I could afford only four, but Flower Girl insisted on throwing in an extra one for free because odd numbers look better, she said. She wrapped the five of them with some green leafy stuff and they looked really good. She even tied a ribbon around them and I made the connection that she might be to flowers what William is to books. When I paid her, she gave me a card from the flower shop and said, "And if it doesn't work out with cheerful-enthusiastic-sweet-smart-hot, you know where to find me." That really surprised me. I didn't think I would be her type except we both like to read.

I arrived at Alicia's house about ten minutes early and I didn't want to seem so eager, so I stood outside and gave myself a little pep talk. Maybe an "anti-pep" talk was more accurate since I planned to stick to my word and be a perfect gentleman. Dinner would be no problem, but the movie might be challenging. An action-packed movie would be best. I knew not to get too comfortable on the couch. "Stay vertical" would be my mantra. And I'd better leave right after the movie, even though I knew I wouldn't want to. It was better to take it slow now and let her continue to warm up to me as she seemed to be doing anyway. Patience.

I pushed the intercom button next to the tiny "A. Klaer" sign so she could buzz me in, and she told me what apartment to come to on the second floor. She opened the door before I knocked and exclaimed, "Flowers! You are so sweet." Alicia hugged me and gave me a quick kiss and invited me in. Immediately my senses were overloaded by sounds, sights, and smells, but it was the sight of Alicia in yoga pants that made my heart race. The dreaded yoga pants. Some people might think that this is not a very sexy look, barefoot Alicia with a tight little t-shirt and yoga pants, but I know different. When a girl is in yoga pants she feels extra comfortable and sits with her knees pulled up and lounges about in a way she would never do in a dress. Then there is the matter of curves, which Alicia has plenty of. Yoga pants and a tight shirt show every hill and valley. But it is the lack of a waist band that is the most problematic, since there are no buttons or zippers to contend with. It is way too easy to slip your hands down a pair of yoga pants. Keeping my hands out of Alicia's pants was going to be more challenging than eating two Carnegie sandwiches.

I watched her bend over and find a vase for the flowers. Alicia was making some type of stir fry and she had a big wok on the stove, a rice steamer on the counter, and a chopping board with an array of colorful vegetables. "Wow, I thought you said you weren't much of a cook!"

"I'm really not," she answered. "I basically just steam rice and chop vegetables. I use sauce out of a jar."

"What about meat?"

"I am going to sauté some chicken before I add the vegetables. Sometimes I make it with tofu and use a different sauce. Do you like tofu?"

"I don't think I've ever had it." I was eating raw chopped bell peppers off the cutting board. "I like your apartment." I looked around and saw that it was as small as mine, except maybe a little longer and way cooler. She had an exposed brick wall and the perpendicular wall had long narrow windows which opened onto a fire escape. The small kitchen was open to the living area and had a little breakfast bar with real granite and stools to sit at. She had a futon similar to my new one and a desk with a computer and a bookcase full of things I planned to take a closer look at. Everything was neat, orderly, and new-looking. "Where's your tv?"

"I don't have a tv. We can watch a movie on my computer." There was a large monitor on her desk. I excused myself to use the bathroom and that is where my senses were bombarded by an array of girliness. There was a very fragrant candle burning and everything in there was color-coordinated lavender or white. She had soft and fluffy big plush towels and a thick rug. I felt like I was in a museum of luscious femininity, like I was an intruder in the temple of womanhood. I took my time drying my hands just because her towels were so soft and clean and everything smelt so good.

When I returned, Alicia was busy with the stir fry, so I walked over to that tall bookcase to see what I could learn about Alicia Klaer. The bottom shelf was full of exercise and nutrition books. I noticed she had dumbbells near the shelf and one of those exercise balls, although I have no idea how they are used.

The second shelf was full of textbooks, but the third had novels. Most of them seemed to be girl books, but I was happy to see a copy of *Catcher in The Rye* and *To Kill a Mockingbird*. The two top shelves had photos in frames. They weren't portraits: they were vacation type photos and all portrayed a mom, a dad, and three blonde girls all in amazing outdoor settings, but not posed. "Wow, it looks like your family knows how to have fun."

"You could say that," Alicia laughed and walked over to the bookcase. "Growing up I didn't appreciate it. I'd get back from spring break or summer vacations and all my friends would talk about the resorts they had visited and about lounging by the pool. My dad would make us carry heavy packs and go trekking for miles, places like Yosemite." Alicia picked up the frame that showed her in front of Half Dome. "I fantasized about staying in a hotel, lounging by a pool and being around other teenagers, especially boys! But now I realize I am pretty lucky to have seen with my own eyes places most people only see in books or if they do visit, they barely scratch the surface. Like the Grand Canyon. Millions of tourists go to the edge and look down, but my dad made us hike down into it and sleep in the canyon for two nights."

"I should call you 'Adventure Barbie,'" I joked, picking up a photo of her in a raft with her family.

"Yeah, if Barbie were short and chubby."

"Hey, did you just call my girl chubby?" I looked at her like I was mad.

Alicia stared back at me and answered, "I dunno, did you just call me your girl?" We were in a stare down, eyes locked. Alicia raised an eyebrow, which looked more sexy than intellectual on her. She had a smirk and a hand on her hip.

"What if I did? Would that be a problem?" I can't raise an eyebrow, but I do have a smirk.

"Well, it would depend on what you meant by it." We stared at each other for about five seconds and I wasn't sure how to answer. We were in a game of emotional poker and I wasn't sure if I should lay my cards down. Alicia folded first with a giggle, "Does 'my girl' mean 'girlfriend'?"

"Well,..." My answer had to be slow and methodical. "That would be presumptuous of me, don't you think?"

"Hmmmm. Not really. I mean, we do talk everyday and now you are in my apartment and I'm cooking dinner for you, so no, I don't think that would be too presumptuous at all."

"So you are saying it is okay for me to refer to you as my girlfriend?"

Alicia smiled coyly, "Well, I'd like that. But only if I can call you my boyfriend."

"Well, okay, I guess I can cancel all those other dates I had lined up," I teased her and she smacked my arm, "Do we need to shake on it?"

"We need to kiss on it," she said, wrapping her arms around me.

And so I ate my girlfriend's cooking and it was the first home-cooked meal I had eaten in a few years. I thought it was amazing, but Alicia seemed self-conscious about it and kept saying she could do better next time. She drank some wine and had beer for me, but I was careful to limit myself to two drinks. I was committed to staying sharp and keeping my hands out of those yoga pants. Things were heating up at a good pace and I didn't want to push my luck. I was pretty damn lucky and I knew it. But we did start kissing during the movie and we made out for a really long time. At one point she crawled up on my lap and... okay, I did get my hands down those damn easy-access yoga pants and felt her bare bottom, her nice smooth butt. Alright, I admit I felt her tits too, but not under her bra, and the fact that I was able to stop there and… well, I had to kick her off my lap. I told her nicely of course. I said, "Alicia, it is getting really hard for me to be a gentleman with you straddling my lap."

"Oh, sorry!" She jumped off me and straightened her shirt and hair.

"Oh, I don't mind at all. You can sit on my lap anytime you want. Just know that you were making it hard on me."

"Oh, I felt it," she smiled. "It was hard on me too," she giggled and kissed me but sat down at my side on the futon and we tried to watch the rest of the movie. It would be really difficult for me to leave before midnight like I promised, but I knew she had to study in the morning and I was really conscious of the fact that school is her priority and I don't want her thinking she can't have a boyfriend too. Plus, she asked to come to my soccer game again. I was happy about that because it would probably be my last chance to play for a while since Don signed that big contract and said we'd be working Saturdays starting the next week.

I kissed Alicia goodbye at the door, checked my phone, and saw that it was 11:53 p.m. I felt like a gentleman. A punctual gentleman and pretty good guy.

At the next morning's soccer match I was on fire. Marcus teased me about showing off for my girlfriend, but Alicia wasn't even there yet. The truth is I was in a very good mood. Plus, I had been sleeping and eating regularly and not stressing about money as much as before. I still didn't have much extra cash, but I knew a bunch of overtime was in my future.

I asked Alicia if she wanted me to plan something for after

the game, but she said she would bring lunch again and we could just do whatever. I have always loved Saturdays, but I really loved Saturdays even more now. The day was starting to signify for me what it did for most people: a well-deserved break from the workweek and a chance to spend time with someone I care about.

About two-thirds into the game I expected to see Alicia but she still had not shown up and I tried to stay focused. She wasn't there at the end of the game either and I was starting to wonder what had happened. I said goodbye to Marcus and Gloria and got my phone out of my backpack. There were two texts from Alicia, the first about the study group running late, the second saying she was on her way. Then I heard her call my name. I turned and saw her walking towards me and I muttered a spontaneous prayer: "Thank you, God, for summer time, for short shorts, and for Alicia Klaer." We hugged for a long time, the kind of hug when someone gets off a plane or ship coming back from war. "I'm so glad to see you," she beamed up at me. I still couldn't understand why this beautiful girl was so crazy about me, but I wasn't about to point out the flaws in her taste. She'd probably come to her senses, but I was determined to enjoy her temporary insanity until then.

She asked if I was hungry and I said, "Yeah, I've been hungry pretty much the whole year except when we left Carnegie's."

"What? You were hungry last night?"

"A little," I admitted. "I mean, the food you made was really good, but I was hungry again by midnight."

"Oh, Ray, I wish you'd said something! I don't know how much food to cook for a guy." She was turning red and looking sad.

"Oh, it was plenty, Alicia. I didn't mean that. But you

know what they say about Chinese food: you're hungry again an hour later."

Alicia was still looking disappointed as she said, "And I didn't even have time to pack lunch today."

"Aww, don't worry about that. I'll just get a hot dog." Then I remembered she probably didn't eat hot dogs so I said, "Or we can go out to lunch somewhere." I actually had a twenty and a ten in my wallet.

"Oh, I'm not even hungry. While you were playing soccer, I was eating snacks and just sitting on my butt studying."

"Speaking of your cute butt," I pulled her ear close to my mouth, "I was thinking about it all night."

Alicia was turning red and did this cute thing where she covered her smile with her hand. "You should eat, Ray. There's a hot dog cart."

"Sure you don't mind? I am hungry."

"No, of course! Eat two!" She laughed.

"I was thinking three."

We sat on the grass talking while I inhaled three hot dogs and Alicia sipped on a diet coke. She told me about her study group of three girls and two guys. I started to wonder about the guys she spent so much time with and what they were like, but she told me and I didn't have to ask. One was nice, but older and married. The other guy she didn't care for but tolerated because it really helped to study in a group. She explained that they spent the morning creating practice test questions and it was way better than studying alone. "I always get distracted after about an hour, but with the peer pressure of the group, I have to stick it out. I have to study again sometime today or tonight and meet up with them again tomorrow."

"Where do you study?"

"Oh, sometimes at home, but I like to go to coffee shops or the library. I get too distracted at home alone."

"Do you go to the St. Agnes branch?" It is the library closest to her place.

"Usually. I like Mid-Manhattan too, but a lot of homeless people hang out there and it smells bad."

"Yeah, but not so much in the summertime. It's just the winter when they're trying to stay warm."

"Oh yeah, I never thought of that. I haven't been there in a while."

"I'm friends with the librarian," I told her. I hoped it was okay to call William my friend.

"Oh, really?" Alicia asked, smiling at me. "Do you have one of those hottie-librarian fetishes?"

I laughed thinking of course she thought the librarian was a woman. I told her about William and she seemed intrigued. "Hey," I said, "I have an idea. Since you have to study some more, do you want to go to the library together? I need to return a book anyway and can hang out and read while you study."

"Are you serious? You'd hang out at the library with me on a Saturday?"

"Alicia, I fucking love libraries." I admitted in a dead pan voice. She laughed in response, "I don't think I've ever heard you cuss before."

"Sorry about that," I said.

"Oh, don't be. I just had no idea you were so passionate about libraries." Alicia was laughing at me and I didn't mind at all. It was better to let her think I was a book nerd instead of one of the homeless guys seeking shelter and stinking up the place.

We walked back towards our apartments. I wanted to take a shower and Alicia needed to get her books, so we agreed to meet at the subway station in an hour.

The train was full and we had to stand. I couldn't tell if Alicia was rubbing her butt into me on purpose or by accident, but either way I liked it. It seemed odd that our relationship had so much to do with the subway station, but this was the first time we actually rode the subway together. On weekdays the cars were loaded with professionals, but today the crowd included three guys who had already started partying and were being loud and obnoxious. I started feeling really protective of Alicia, thinking about how much time she spends on the subway alone and walking around by herself. I was wishing I could be there to protect her all the time, although logically I knew she got along just fine before she met me.

When we got to the library, I didn't see William. It would make sense that he wouldn't work on Saturdays, so I returned my book and asked where I could find *The Buffalo Hunter*, the book Flower Girl was reading. I did not notice who the author was or I could have found it myself. The girl acted put out at my question and said I could use one of the help computers to find it. She'd never be as popular as William, even though she was pretty.

Alicia was sitting at a table and I sat across from her as I started reading. I usually know on the first page if I am going to like a book and this one grabbed me right from the start. I'd be content reading for hours, but Alicia's homework must not have been as interesting as my book because after a few minutes she slipped a piece of paper across the table at me and it said, "Stop it! You're distracting me."

I tried shrugging my shoulders and raising my hands in the air as if to say, "What?" But she wasn't looking at me, so I picked up her pen and wrote back, "I'm not doing anything."

Alicia smiled and didn't look up, but wrote back, "You are too. You must be releasing pheromones. I can't even think straight. I want to crawl on your lap and kiss you."

Damn, she was hot. A little ball of hot passion packaged in a girl-next-door look, talking about seducing me in the library. I couldn't stand up now even if I wanted to, not after that reminder of her sitting on my lap. I did some long division in my head before writing her back.

"I am going to go sit in a chair by the window for one hour. I want you to do as much homework as you can during that time. Then I am going to pull you into the book stacks and kiss you. But not before then, so quit distracting me." I pushed the note to her and went and sat down by the window. That girl had better not get a "B" and blame it on me.

I was really into *The Buffalo Hunter* and didn't notice when William came and sat across from me. "Hello, Raymond, what a splendid evening for reading, much like all others. May I?" He held out his hand to have a look at my book.

I handed it to him and he said, "Hmmm, this author tends to favor the horror genre."

"This one isn't horror, although the guy is a bit creepy. And it takes place in Manhattan."

Both eyebrows arched up as William studied the book

cover. He was wearing a nice dark suit and light shirt, but no tie.

"Do you have to dress up for work on Saturdays?"

"Oh, I'm not working today. I am meeting a date here before whisking her off to the theater."

"Oh yeah, I almost forgot it's a Saturday night. I'm here with my girlfriend. She has to study."

I nodded towards Alicia, who was already looking at us, and I waved.

"Ah, and a vision of loveliness she is. Please make the introductions." We walked over to Alicia and I whispered in a library voice, "This is my friend William I told you about. William, this is Alicia."

He shook her hand but did not let go. Instead he sat down across from her still holding her hand in both of his and never stopped looking her in the eyes. Damn, this guy was intense. He asked her what she was studying and Alicia told him she was working on getting her CPA. They spoke in hushed tones about school stuff that wasn't really that interesting to me, but it was their body language that was starting to irritate the hell out of me. William had his face too close to her and Alicia was smiling and looking shy like she looked at me, then she did that thing where she puts her hand over her mouth to hide her smile and I felt like my blood was about to boil! At that point William released her hand, and looking at me whispered loudly enough for her to hear, "What a treasure you have here, Raymond. I thought you were being effusive, but she is every bit as lovely as you described."

Then he said goodbye and Alicia was smiling and I don't know what kind of voodoo shit he pulled with his words because I was sure I had never mentioned Alicia to him, and I definitely hadn't described her. I gave my head a fast vigorous shake, as if to clear my thoughts and Alicia whispered, "Wow. You were right about him. He is intense and interesting."

"Yeah, women love him," I concurred dryly.

"Well, I prefer my bookworms to be a little more masculine. You know, guys that maybe play soccer, work construction, and have voracious appetites."

"Oh, you do, do you?" My mood rollercoaster was already back on the upswing. "That type of bookworm is very rare, you know."

"I do know that. I got pretty lucky. Has it been an hour yet?"

"Close enough," I answered, then led her into the book stacks for a sneaky make-out session before the next study hour.

When we left the library, Alicia was hungry and asked if I liked Pho. I admitted I didn't know what that was and she said she was about to share one of her favorite things with me. We went to this tiny place near the library. Who knew a girl could get so excited about a bowl of broth with some noodles? It was pretty good, but I would have left hungry if she hadn't suggested I get something called "shabu" as well. Shabu is meat cut really thin, but tasty. The food was cheap and spicy and we both enjoyed it.

We got off the subway at the station where we met and I walked Alicia home. I really didn't have any expectation about what would happen next. It was a busy day and a beautiful night, the stars were out and I was happy to be walking hand in hand with my girlfriend.

She didn't invite me in. Instead we kissed on the stoop and then she told me she had to study all day on Sunday for a big test she had on Monday morning, but after that she could relax. She asked if I could come over again on Monday night.

"Are you going to try to seduce me with your home cooking again?" I teased her.

"I might," she teased back. "Maybe you should bring condoms instead of flowers this time," and she winked at me as she said goodnight. I stood there stunned staring at the door for a few seconds. Did I just imagine it or did Alicia really say to bring condoms instead of flowers? Was she joking? Either way, I knew I would bring them. Hell, I might bring flowers too.

8 - PASTRIES

Sunday morning I woke up with every reason to be in a great mood. I had a beautiful new girlfriend, the apartment to myself, a job with some security, and a whole day in front of me with nothing to do. But it was the nothing-to-do part that was bumming me out. It made me feel like the old Ray, the one who used to roam around all day depressed with no one to talk to. I tried to shake it off and get busy: there were plenty of projects I could work on in my apartment. So I painted one wall, refinished my coffee table, and was in the middle of building a bookshelf out of scrap wood when my phone rang. I expected my dad, but it was Carlos.

"Hey, man! 'Bout time you called me back!" I greeted him.

"Me? You fuckin' don't call me for a whole fuckin' year, then expect me to call you right back? Fuck you."

Whoa, I thought. *That was a lot of f-bombs. Carlos is pissed.*

"Yeah, you're right. I've sort of had my head up my ass this past year."

"What's your fuckin' problem? Have you been pissed at me since I left after we got fired?" He was unloading on me, hard and heavy.

"Naw, man, that wasn't it at all. I probably would have left too, if I had a nice home to go back to." I sat down on my futon. "Remember how I let that guy Thomas move in? Well, he brought this other guy in and the two of them went crazy doing drugs and things got pretty bad around here with them stealing my shit, bringing hookers and junkies home, and all kinds of weird stuff goin' on in this tiny place."

"Shit, man, you didn't do drugs with 'em, did you?"

"Hell no!"

"You could've at least called and said what was goin' on, stupid motherfucker. You want me to come help you evict those motherfuckers or somethin'?"

"They're both gone now. One's in jail, one's in rehab."

"Sounds like a good place for 'em. How're you doin' now?"

"Better. Much better. How 'bout you?"

"Got me a new job and a new girl," Carlos laughed in that cocky way of his. Carlos could swagger with nothing more than the tone of his voice.

The rest of our dialogue slid into our old familiar pattern, just like we used to, except we had a lot of catching up to do. He laughed about how I got my new job and of course about how I met my new girlfriend.

"She came up and hugged you, just because you asked?"

"Yeah… well, I guess I helped her out one time when she dropped a bunch of stuff, but she definitely surprised me. She's still surprising me." I was thinking about how Alicia told me to bring condoms, but I didn't tell Carlos that part. I surprised myself because that was the kind of stuff I would normally tell him.

"Well I hope she ain't no 'false advertiser'," Carlos joked.

I laughed, "Nope, definitely not. She's super-hot, but really sweet too. Hey, Marcus is asking about you all the time."

"Ah, really? That's cool. I should come out for soccer and bring my new girl and meet yours too."

"That'd be cool, 'cept I'm gonna' be working the next few Saturdays. I'm gonna play with a few of the same guys on Tuesdays for a while instead."

"Yeah, well, maybe in a month or so." Carlos went on and updated me on what all our old friends were doing, which sounded like just more of the same old same old. We ended the conversation with Carlos telling me not to go "a whole fuckin' year" without calling him and I laughed and agreed.

When I hung up I saw a text from Alicia. It had a selfie with an accounting book covering the lower half of her face and it said, "Stop distracting me!"

I laughed and wrote back, "Whoever this is, knock it off. I have a girlfriend now."

She sent another selfie, this time one of her butt, with her jeans pulled down. She was wearing a pink thong. Damn.

Surprised again. The caption said, "Recognize me now?"

I wrote back, "I could pick that sweet ass out of any lineup. Why don't you come over and study on my lap?"

"Hahaha. You have to wait until tomorrow," she texted.

"I know. Feel free to keep those pics coming. I miss you." I texted back.

Then she texted me a row of hearts and said she missed me too.

The next morning I was a few minutes early getting to the address Don had given me. He said he wanted to take Lenny and me out to breakfast. "Don't worry, you're on the clock. Just want to go over some stuff." He was in a great mood, but anxious too. Don explained that we needed to finish up a bunch of work this week and start our new job next week. We would be working on a warehouse that was being converted into residential lofts.

"Do you know what this means, Ray?" Lenny asked, elbowing me in the ribs.

I thought about it for a few seconds before answering, "Prosperity?"

For some reason both guys thought this was hilarious and they repeated it a few times, laughing until Lenny answered, "Yeah, prosperity, Ray. It also means we have steady work for the rest of the year, and come winter, we'll be working indoors at the same place everyday instead of freezin' our balls off!"

"And," Don added, "It means we gotta up our game. Lenny, I want you to spend the next week teaching Ray as much as you can about every trade, which ones we're gonna sub out, and what we're gonna do ourselves. Ray might have to supervise some guys and coordinate shit, and hey, Ray, there's gonna be some days where you're holdin' a clipboard instead of a drill."

Our food came and we dug in, but Don kept talking, "And don't forget, both of ya's, you need to set an example for any new guys: no coming in late, no bein' on the phone."

I had to bite my lip at that. Few things irritate me more than being told to do something I am already doing, or not to do something I'm already not doing, but I knew Don was just looking ahead. "I even ordered some t-shirts with collars. They say DT Construction right here," he was rubbing the left side of his chest and he was grinning with pride.

When we got back to the jobsite, Lenny did proceed to explain everything he was doing while trying to rush at the same time. He gave me specific tips for checking other people's work and also what would catch Don's eye. I took some notes and asked a lot of questions and even made a few video clips when he showed me something new. Lenny teased me about studying at night, but I definitely had my mind on other ideas for that particular evening. Alicia's place.

That morning I had texted her wishing her luck on her test and hadn't heard back from her yet. Lenny caught me grinning a few times and asked, "What's so funny?" I didn't want to tell him I was thinking about the picture of Alicia's butt, so I said, "Don was really excited about those t-shirts."

"Yeah well, it's been a hell of a ride for him. It ain't easy being the owner. I wouldn't do it, I got enough stress with my kids." We were tiling the bathroom of an apartment and I really enjoyed it, except for the smell of cutting tile. We barely finished at five o'clock and I finally got a text that read, "Test is over, home from work, come over any time."

I put my tools away and then literally ran home to take a shower.

It takes me about forty-five minutes to walk to Alicia's apartment, and almost as long to take the subway. I prefer walking, especially when it's nice out. I walked by the flower shop and spontaneously decided to pop in. I saw Flower Girl again and she teased me, "Back so soon? Must be love."

"Sorry, but I don't know you that well yet. I think 'like' would be more honest." I teased her back even though I knew what she meant.

Flower Girl smiled and asked if I was on a budget again today. "Always. But today I do want to buy just one rose and I was hoping you could tell me what the different colored roses mean."

"I just know that red is love and I'm pretty sure yellow is sympathy. Let's Google it." She looked at her phone screen and walked over to the buckets of roses. Girls with tattoos are confusing. Flower Girl had this tattoo on her thigh and she was wearing short cut-off jeans and black boots, so of course I was looking at her legs. Or rather her tattoos. It's a mind game they play, giving you permission to look at the art on some private body part. Not that her upper thigh was that private, but I usually wouldn't stare like that.

"I like to write," she noticed my staring. "And I like birds."

"Hmmm. That explains it. Very interesting." Her pale thighs *were* very interesting, and so was the typewriter surrounded by birds.

"Okay, here are the ones we have in stock. Let me see, pink means appreciation, oh, unless it's light pink; that means admiration." She looked at me and I shook my head. "Okay, white means purity or innocence, red means love, of course."

"What about this one?" I pointed to a really cool looking rose, yellow with red tips.

"That," she consulted her phone's screen, "Means friendship and falling in love."

I stared at the flower for a few seconds. Then I picked it up.

"Dammit!" Flower Girl exclaimed. "I guess that means there's no hope for you and me," she laughed like she was joking.

"I guess we were meant to be just friends," I shrugged and gave her my most charming smile.

We walked up to the counter and as she rang me up, I asked, "Do most girls know what the colors of flowers mean?"

"Well, I own a flower shop and I had to look it up. Except red, of course."

"You own this place?"

"Yep. Three years."

"Damn, Tracy. Impressive."

"Did I tell you my name?"

"It was on your business card, but it didn't say you own the place. My name is Ray."

"Your name is Ray and you're falling in love," she sighed, handing me my change. "Well, it's good for business."

I thanked Tracy the Flower-Girl-business-owner and continued on my way.

In front of Alicia's apartment I gave myself the anti-pep talk. Just because I had condoms in my pocket didn't mean I would for sure get to use them. I would just take it slow, see what happened, and be a gentleman. I rang the intercom.

Alicia buzzed me in and once again opened the door before I knocked. When she saw that I was holding a flower, her face fell.

"What's wrong?" I asked.

"Does this mean you don't want to have sex with me?"

"What?" I couldn't believe my ears until I remembered she said to bring condoms *instead* of flowers. "Oh, I brought both."

Alicia looked mortified and I hugged her. "Oh my god, I am so embarrassed. I can't believe I just blurted that out."

I hugged here even more closely and laughing said, "Baby, you really should familiarize yourself with the meaning of flowers. I'll bet there isn't a single flower that says 'No sex for you'."

"Maybe some sort of cactus." She was at least smiling now, but her face was redder than I'd ever seen. I lifted her chin up with my hand and kissed her tenderly.

"How did your test go?" I asked.

"Oh my god, it was so hard, Ray. I won't know my grade until tomorrow." I noticed I was starting to feel anxious about her grades myself. "Are you hungry?" she asked.

"Always."

"I made a salad and it will just take ten minutes to make pasta."

"Thank you. I'd like that."

I sat on the stool at her breakfast bar and watched her put a pot of water on the stove, and then she put the rose in a vase. "You're spoiling me," she smiled and came to me where I was sitting and stood between my legs and kissed me. I really like how affectionate and passionate she is, that she doesn't wait for me to kiss her every time. "We don't have to do it, you know."

As I looked at her, not really sure how to respond, she went on, "I mean, I told you to bring condoms just in case, but I…

Time to shut her up with a kiss—the kind that wouldn't let her talk for a while, the kind that would leave her breathless. When I finally let her loose, she backed up and had lost her insecure look. She had a sexy expression and a completely confident demeanor as she stated, "I'm going to finish cooking." I watched her slide some dry pasta into the water and take a salad out of the fridge. "Do you want one of your beers?"

"Sure, I'd love one."

Alicia had some music playing and a few candles burning. She was wearing shorts and a tank top. It was a warm night, but she had a fan by the open window. She handed me a beer and I drank it from the cold bottle while she puttered in the kitchen. I loved watching her, seeing her move and bend and concentrate on what she was doing. She took a salad she had already prepared out of the fridge and scooped some onto two plates and placed them on the bar. I couldn't remember the last time I had eaten salad; it sure wasn't something I would make for myself. It was full of tiny chopped vegetables, such as cucumber, tomatoes, celery, and carrots. Everything tasted fresh and crunchy. Next Alicia brought me a plate of pasta with marinara sauce, but she just ate salad saying she wasn't that hungry. I noticed that she had scratches on the back of her hand again and asked about it. "Oh, I think it's from filing things at work. You know, sticking my hands down into file drawers and sometimes the documents are stapled together."

"Whoa," I said holding up my own hands and looking at them. "Who would have guessed accounting could be so much more hazardous than construction?" Alicia laughed and we started eating. I dug into my pasta and said, "You know, I think you are the one spoiling me. I can't believe I am eating my second home-cooked meal in a week," I told her.

"If you call this cooking," she laughed, gesturing to the plate of pasta.

"Oh, I do."

We talked about our days as we ate and when we finished Alicia took the dishes and put them in the sink. I offered to wash them, but she declined. Instead, she offered to download some music onto my phone from her computer. Alicia has a ton of different types of music and I like some of it, but not all. I took off my shoes and socks and we both lay down on her plush throw rug. Alicia was already barefoot and I admired her pink toenails before saying, "Don't put any of that country stuff on my phone." I said it like I was teasing, but I was serious.

"What, you mean bluegrass?"

"Yeah, I don't have the hillbilly gene."

"Actually, I think you do, since you're half Irish." I looked at her expectantly and she went on, "Irish immigrants settled in the Appalachian Mountains and brought their instruments, at least the ones they could carry across the mountains. Banjos, fiddles, mandolins. They played Irish folk tunes that eventually morphed into what we now know as bluegrass."

"Okay Miss Wikipedia, but I think my Hispanic side is dominant when it comes to music."

Alicia slipped into a high falsetto and said in a kind of sing-song, "But you must embrace all aspects of your entire persona as a dynamic whole. That combination makes you the lovable being that you are."

I looked at her in surprise and she said, "Sorry. That was my therapist talking."

"You have a therapist?"

"Well, not right now."

"Why would you need therapy?"

"You have no idea," she laughed, then said, "Hey, I really want you to give bluegrass a try. One of my favorite bands is going to play here in a few months and I'd love it if you would go with me."

"Will I need to grow a beard?" I joked with her, stroking my chin. "Of course I'll go with you. Put a few songs on my phone and I'll see if I can get into it."

"So you will embrace your inner hillbilly?" She teased. She was lying on her side now and I asked, "Would you like to be embraced by my inner hillbilly, or would you rather get acquainted with my Latin lover side?"

"Oooo, no contest, Rico Suave. I want it spicy!" She laughed but I turned solemn and stroked her cheek with my hand.

"I'm really glad I met you," I said, lightly stroking her cheek with my forefinger.

"Me too," she answered, matching my gaze and change of tone.

"I wasn't expecting to meet anybody. You kind of blindsided me. But you have no idea how glad I am that you came along."

"I feel the same way."

I was looking into her big blue eyes with the long lashes that sparked out, and was stroking her soft cheek, and I felt like I should say something else, but didn't know what. So, I lowered my mouth to hers and kissed her gently. She let out a sigh and kissed me back. I parted my lips and let our tongues meet and gently swirled mine around hers. We were both on our sides, up on one elbow and I used my other hand to dig into her hair at the nape of her neck and pull her in closer and kiss her deeply. Our breathing quickened and Alicia threw her leg over me. I responded by lowering my hand all the way to her sweet ass and pulling her into me even more closely, so that I was really pressing into her and kissing her the whole time, alternating between soft, gentle, tender kisses and deep, urgent kisses.

There was no way to hide how turned on I was and I didn't bother. Instead I rolled onto my back and pulled Alicia over on top of me and let my hands explore her beautiful body. Her hair hung around me like a curtain and she continued to kiss me while I massaged the curviness of her sexy bottom and admitted, "I am completely crazy over this butt." She responded with a smile and by grinding herself into me. I was really feeling the urge to shed my jeans, but then Alicia sat up and pulled her tank top off in the swiftest sexiest move I have ever seen.

She was wearing a lacy bra. I knew she had nice tits but

I'd never actually seen them. Her bra was a light pink color and sheer enough I could see her nipples. I reached up and felt one through the fabric with my thumb and she smiled shyly at me. I used both hands to massage her breasts and then she reached behind her back and unhooked the bra and tossed it aside, revealing the most gorgeous sight I could ever imagine. Perfect symmetry and shape, soft yet firm, round breasts partially covered by her pretty blonde hair, and the most gorgeous nipples, which I was aching to taste. "You are so beautiful," I said as I marveled at the sight of my brown-skinned hands massaging her pale breasts. She leaned back and tossed her hair backward and asked me to take my shirt off too.

I sat up and pulled my shirt off and realigned my body so I was now sitting with my back against her futon and she was straddling me. We were still in our pants and shorts, but our bare chests were pressed together and I kissed her neck, and then down to her hard nipple that was begging for my mouth. Alicia gasped and I felt her arch her back again as she put a hand on the back of my head. I was overwhelmed with passion and became greedy with her breasts, using both my hands and mouth to bring more of her to me. I switched sides and continued using both hands, feeling the weight of her breasts in my palms, feeling her other nipple harden in response to my mouth and lips and tongue. I was starting to ache from straining against my jeans and her weight on me and I gently lifted her butt up and back and set her down between my legs and laid her down on her back.

Now I was looking down at her pretty face that looked back up at me shy and expectant. "May I please have permission to remove your pesky shorts?"

"Yes! Get them off!" she almost begged, "And remove your pesky pants too."

And so I did, unveiling my desire for her and revealing her

lacy panties to me. I lay back on top of her, careful not to apply all my weight, and it felt so good to feel her body next to mine, her soft pale skin against my light brown skin, the entire length of us, ankles touching, knees touching, thighs touching, abdomen and chest pressing together, and me between her legs pushing into that hot magnet that wanted to draw me in. My hands roamed her entire body, feeling every inch of her skin. I wanted to explore every surface on her body, I wanted to taste every inch. I kissed her shoulder and even down her arm. I had never wanted to kiss a girl's arm before, never wanted to take my time like this. It was as if we had all the time in the world and I knew where we were going, but getting there was better than I had ever imagined.

As I continued to roam with my mouth, I lowered one hand down to her butt and pulled her into me, literally aching in such a good way. Without removing her panties, I allowed my hand to explore further down her crack and between her legs, confirming that she was incredibly hot. A moan escaped my lips when the tips of my two fingers met her wetness. Alicia's breathing was ragged and she was grinding her hips into me from below, which allowed me further access to enter her wetness with my finger and feel for the first time how hot and smooth and slippery she was. I slid a finger all the way inside her and she gasped and moaned my name and I felt her nails dig into my back.

I lifted myself to look down at her and she gave me the most wicked but charming smile, the most beautiful smile ever with her hair now all wild and her breasts free. I admired the curve of her small waist meeting the flare of her ample hips and the lacy panties that were now very much in my way.

"May I?" I asked, as I pulled them away from her hip. Alicia bit her lip and nodded at me, then lifted her hips so I could remove her lacy pink panties. I took my time, stopping to kiss and stroke her legs on the way down, then slowly kissed them all the way back up. I stopped at the apex of her legs and slid a finger back into her. She was up on her elbows watching me, biting her lip again. I wanted to taste that sweet nectar between her legs and I looked up at her for any indication, but she let her head fall back and closed her eyes in response to my finger sliding slowly in and out of her. I decided to take that as a yes.

And so I tasted my girlfriend for the first time and even though I wasn't touching myself, my cock jumped in response as I heard a soft murmur "Oh my god, Ray, oh my god," and she tasted salty and sweet and delicious and I continued to lick her and finger her and worship her beautiful body.

She was getting incredibly squirmy again, and while putting a hand on the back of my head, she was pulling me in and gently undulating her hips. I wanted to stay there forever, but she abruptly sat up and commanded, "Come here!" with urgency, so I crawled over her not sure if I should kiss her right then but she hungrily kissed me from below and began stroking me through my shorts. I was on my elbows letting her caress the length of my shaft with her delicate but deliberate touch and then she reached her hand inside my boxer shorts and wrapped it around me, firmly.

Now I was the one panting as she pushed me over onto my side and pulled my boxers down. I lifted my hips for her and she lowered her mouth on me deftly and completely, and I let out a moan. The blond cloud of hair all over my groin blocked my view, and so scooping up her hair ponytail fashion, I was able to watch her beautiful mouth slide over me. It was almost too much. I half considered distracting myself with math problems in my head, but then I went back to watching her and feeling her warm, wet mouth embrace me over and over, working in tandem with her strong but delicate and talented hand.

I could have stayed like that all night. I looked around and the room was dark now, except for the burning candles Alicia had placed and one small light from the kitchen. The vanilla smell of the candles was in the background: it was mostly us I could smell. Alicia had left music playing softly on the computer. I gazed down at her loving me, caressing me with her mouth, and realized she would go on until I stopped her. She was so sexy and so eager to please me, but I really wanted to put myself on top of her and inside of her. I didn't say anything, just gently guided her head up and off me and pulled her up towards me. "What's wrong? Didn't you like it?"

I had to laugh at that, "Baby, I liked it a little too much." *How could this incredibly sexy woman be so insecure sometimes?* I wondered. Alicia grinned and crawled on top of me and began kissing me, which was a little dangerous because we both were nude and I didn't have a condom on yet. I held her by the waist and rolled over on top of her and kissed her mouth, her neck, and back down to her chest. She had her legs wrapped around me and it was tough to break away long enough to grab my pants and get a condom out of my pocket. I took my time putting it on, trying to allow myself to calm a bit, while Alicia just smiled at me the whole time until I was ready.

She had her knees bent and I was on my knees between her legs as I lowered my body on top of hers and kissed her one more time before placing myself at her entrance. I lifted my head to look at her face and make sure, "Is this okay?"

"More than okay," she answered. As I slowly entered her we never broke eye contact. I took my time and slid in as slowly as I could, feeling her tight grip squeezing me, but allowing me all the way in until I was as deep as I could possibly go. I paused, still looking in her eyes and said, "Wow." I couldn't believe I was inside Alicia, all the way inside her, this beautiful girl gazing back with love and passion in her eyes. She said, "You feel so amazing inside me." Her hands were on my lower back, stroking me, and she lowered both hands down to my ass and pulled me even closer. I didn't move my body, just gently kissed her lips and held myself all the way in, buying some time, trying not to be too excited and to just enjoy the feeling of her wrapped around me, then I slowly slid back out, almost completely but not all the way, and slid back in. Alicia gasped and then giggled as if embarrassed by her own passion as I slid out and back again. Then she moaned and I really got lost in feeling her, kissing her, and touching her, massaging her breast with my hand, her neck with my mouth and pushing into her and reveling in that tight embrace that felt so good that I had to divide one hundred and one by seven, then come back to the moment. Alicia was definitely pushing back into me, never passive. We were doing this together and… fourteen with a remainder of three… and I slowed because I was getting too close, but she didn't slow: she was kissing my neck and lifting her hips off the floor and pulling me in with her two hands on my ass.

I was not in charge anymore, even though I was on top. Alicia was squeezing and pulling on me and I couldn't even think up a math problem if I wanted to. I wanted this to last forever but Alicia was moaning and squeezing me until all of her muscles started contracting, everywhere. I stopped fighting it and enjoyed the sensation of her pulsating and it sent me over the edge of no return and I felt my own release coming as I crested the peak and plunged into the inevitable slide into orgasmic bliss. With Alicia moaning my name in my ear I exploded into her and felt my own jerking and contracting and I was moaning too, and still pushing into her, pulling back and pushing as my cum went on and on and on until every last quiver subsided and I relaxed my body onto hers, but still holding my weight up, and Alicia shuddered and then giggled, and said, "So… chemistry is good, right?"

"Chemistry is very good," I laughed, and gently pulled out and rolled over to my side with her still in my arms.

"I'm sorry I didn't last very long, it's been awhile and…."

"Alicia, did you seriously just apologize for cumming too

fast? Oh my god, baby, you are my dream girl." I laughed and kissed her. "That was so amazing, I can't even begin to tell you."

"Did you really just call me your 'dream girl'?" Alicia smiled and looked at me with big eyes.

"Well, that wasn't exactly accurate. I could have never dreamt I'd be this lucky."

Alicia squeezed me really tight and tried to tell me she was the lucky one. What a silly girl. "Please say you're spending the night with me."

"I am." I squeezed her back. I had the foresight to put my toothbrush, drill, and a clean shirt in my backpack. I kissed her once more and got up to use the bathroom and when I stood, Alicia started laughing. I turned around to see what was so funny and she had her hand over her mouth and tears in her eyes as she laughed, "I am so sorry!"

"Why?"

"I left claw marks on your back."

"Really?" I looked over my own shoulder, but of course I didn't see anything.

"Didn't that hurt? I'm so sorry."

"No. I must have liked it, or else there was too much sensation below my waist to even notice."

"Well please don't take off your shirt at soccer or work or anything. I'd be so embarrassed."

I laughed and told her not to worry about it. I liked my "battle scars" anyway. I went to the bathroom to clean up and when I returned Alicia had made the futon up with blankets and pillows. Then she took a turn in the bathroom and came back wearing a tank top and panties, an ensemble that is my second favorite after nudity.

We lay on our sides and kissed and caressed each other and talked until it was nearly midnight. I had to work in the morning and Alicia had school, so she turned off the music and blew out the last candle. We said goodnight and were lying on our sides in a spoon position with Alicia's butt pressed up against my groin. I felt so good and content, but I was getting hard again and I knew I wouldn't be able to sleep. She felt it too and instead of pulling away, began moving her hips and massaging me with her butt. Damn, she felt good. My hand slipped under her tank top and felt her breast. Her nipple was already hard and Alicia interrupted my thoughts with, "I hope you brought more than one condom."

I laughed and confirmed that I had and paused to get one from my pants. I went back to where I was and this time Alicia reached her hand back and placed me at the right angle to enter her from behind. "Dream Girl" is what I was thinking as I entered her for the second time. God, I love this position. I lifted her upper leg and put it over me and used one hand between her legs to make sure she was getting rubbed in the right spot, and she moaned her approval. I was amazed at how sexy she was; I didn't expect her to be so incredibly responsive and to enjoy it as much as I did: that didn't even seem possible. I've never had this feeling with other girls: they often seemed like they were acting or doing it mostly for me. Alicia seemed as hungry for it as I was and I kept thinking "Dream Girl" as my hands explored her body while I made love to her for the second time. We were able to go a lot more slowly this time and to last a lot longer, but again when I felt her muscles start contracting and her moaning got louder, I couldn't hold back any longer and came with her and shuddered with her and relaxed with her into a deep sleep.

I awoke before my phone alarm went off and smiled to myself thinking about the night before. Alicia was asleep on her side with a leg thrown over me and I was tempted to wake her up, but I had to pee so I got up and used the bathroom. I decided to wake her up with some coffee, so I stopped in the kitchen to start brewing it, still marveling at how lucky I was. Everything in her kitchen was well organized, so it was easy to find the filters in a jar next to the coffee maker and the ground beans in the fridge. I used the last of her coffee and thought I should tell her and maybe bring some next time as well. I looked for a trash can for disposing of the empty bag and found one under the sink, but it was full so I pulled it out to push down the contents.

Strangely, it was full of pastry boxes, the cheap kind from the grocery store. *That's weird*, I thought, *Alicia doesn't eat this shit.* I stood there in my boxers staring at the trash can trying to sort this out. Did she have a guy over, some donut-loving motherfucker? Maybe her study group came to her house and they're the ones who eat like this.

"What are you doing?" Alicia was standing in the kitchen doorway in her panties and tank top with messy hair.

"Making coffee," I answered, but she looked pissed or horrified – I couldn't tell which – as she glanced at the trash can.

"Are you snooping? What are you doing?" Was that panic in her voice?

"Relax. I'm just making coffee."

"Don't tell me to relax!" She snapped. She was actually shaking. She stepped towards the trash can and pushed it back in under the sink, closed the cabinet door and spun around. Then she just stared at me with her lips drawn tight and her chin out. I couldn't understand what she was freaking out about – unless maybe she did have something to feel guilty about.

"What's up with all those pastry boxes?" I asked.

Alicia didn't answer; she just stared back at me.

I repeated the question and even gave her a way out. "Did you have people over or something?"

"I think you'd better go now, Ray." She was glaring at me, and I was stunned.

"What?"

She didn't move or answer. I couldn't believe this. How had things gone so bad? What was she hiding?

"No," I answered firmly. "That's bullshit, Alicia. I didn't do anything wrong. We had a great night last night. Why are you turning on me?"

Alicia continued to just stare at me, deadpan.

"Talk to me Alicia. Tell me what's up." I stepped closer and put my hands on her hips. Her lip was trembling and her eyes were filling with tears. I was really scared about what she might say.

"Who ate all that?"

Her eyes darted away and then back to my face. Her expression changed from anger, to fear, to sadness as she sighed and whispered, "I did." Then she turned her back on me and covered her face with her hands.

"What?" I was confused. "Baby, how could you eat all that? I've never seen you eat like that."

Her shoulders were shaking and I realized she was sobbing

silently into her hands. I rubbed her back and spoke to her gently, "Alicia, you're scaring me. Please tell me what's going on."

She was quiet for a few seconds then mumbled something so softly I couldn't hear it. I brought my ear closer to her and asked her to repeat it, "I ate it all, Ray. I can eat that much because I throw it up afterwards."

I stood there in stunned silence. I had heard about girls doing that, but had never known anyone who actually did. Besides, Alicia is twenty-four years old. Isn't that something you outgrow, like binge drinking? I didn't understand; she seemed so… together. She was crying softly into her hands and still wouldn't look at me. "Sometimes I get really stressed out. And I eat too much and I feel like shit afterwards and I hate myself, and oh god, I'm so sorry…." She was sobbing again now and I turned her around gently, held her in my arms, and placed her head on my chest. I didn't make her look at me. I just held her and stroked her back.

"Alicia, you don't have to apologize to me." I stroked her silky hair and said it again. "Don't apologize to me, okay? And don't worry about what I think: I'm crazy about you. But, Alicia, you have to stop doing this; it is so unhealthy. Isn't there something else you can do when you feel stressed out?"

"I used to run and that helps," she whispered.

"Good. What else?" I asked.

"I can call you?" she asked.

"Of course you can. But what if I'm working? What else can you do?"

"I don't know, Ray… I can… maybe try meditating?"

I laughed, "I don't know much about that, but yeah, you need to do something else besides eat and throw up."

"I know, Ray, I know. I'm so sorry. I'm so ashamed of myself. I hate that you know this about me."

"Quit saying you're sorry. You are not doing this to me, but you are doing this to my girlfriend and I care about you so much. Alicia, you can't do this. You're my dream girl."

"Still? After all this?" She spoke in a tiny voice, looking up at me.

"Oh baby, of course, this doesn't change how I feel about you." I held her for a long time, and then I kissed her on her forehead, on her face, then tenderly on her mouth, a slow passionate kiss that became sexier until I felt my arousal stirring and hoped it wasn't entirely inappropriate, but Alicia felt it too and responded by dropping a hand down and stroking me through my boxers. "Grrrrrr," I let out something that sounded like a low growl – there is just something about the morning time – and Alicia whispered, "Let's keep some condoms in a kitchen drawer too." I laughed. She obviously wanted to stay in the kitchen, so I told her to wait just a second while I got another out of my pants.

When I came back she had removed her panties and was sitting on the kitchen counter, my dream girl, and at the perfect height too. As I approached her, she wrapped her sexy legs around me. We made love in the kitchen, with me standing and Alicia on the counter top, and when we both came I gazed into her eyes and looked at her pretty face. She was crying again. I asked, "Are you okay?"

"Yes," she said quietly. "Thank you for not leaving when I told you to. Thank you for not leaving me."

"Baby, I'm not going anywhere." Then I glanced at the kitchen clock out of the corner of my eye and said, "Oh fuck, Alicia! Look what time it is! I'm going to be late for work!"

We both pulled our underwear on and began the mad scramble to get ready and out the door, forgetting all about the coffee. I dressed and brushed my teeth and was ready to bolt out the door in two minutes. I kissed Alicia on the run, but still remembered to say how much I enjoyed her and to thank her for cooking for me, but she was pushing me out the door saying, "Don't be late, don't worry, I'm okay. We'll talk later," and I ran down the steps. It was already eight o'clock and I was going to be late to work. Fuck!

9 - SALSA

Don and Lenny were both standing on the sidewalk at the jobsite when I got there at 8:20 a.m. There was a refrigerator on a dolly and they were obviously waiting for me to help get it upstairs. Don started yelling as soon as he saw me, "What the hell? Didn't I just tell you not to be late and the very next day you're late! What the fuck? Was I talkin' outta the side of my neck or somethin'? Guys are gonna be lookin' at you and you're comin' in late like this?" Don stopped to wipe his sweaty brow with a bandana. It was already hot and humid. "What if I was payin' guys standin' around waitin' on you? This is bullshit!

"I'm sorry, Don. It won't happen again," I answered calmly.

"What?" Don looked at me totally confused, so I went on, "Sorry I let you down."

Don continued to stare at me in bewilderment, and then he started yelling again, "Oh, so I'm the bad guy? You're the one who's fuckin' late and I'm made out to be the asshole?"

"No, not at all. I was totally in the wrong," I again answered calmly, hoping this conversation would be over soon so I could get to work.

Don shook his head and told me just to help get the fridge up the stairs. The three of us manhandled it up two flights of stairs and by the time we got it up and into the tiny kitchen, we were all dripping with perspiration. Don told me to hook the water line to the ice maker and I heard him and Lenny mumbling in the other room. It wasn't just the humidity causing me to sweat.

When I finished with the fridge, I went hunting for Don to find out what he wanted me to do next. He was standing next to the truck talking on the phone and held up a finger signaling me to wait a minute. When he hung up he looked me up and down and said, "Look, Ray, you're a nice kid. That's the problem. Too nice. Next week we're gonna have a few new guys startin' up and you can't act like that."

"I won't be late again. I'm sorry, Don."

"Dammit, Ray, don't you get it? That's exactly what I'm talkin' about right there. Quit bein' so god damned polite or the guys are gonna eat you up. This is a construction site! You're already too young and too green to be in charge. They hear you talkin' like that and they're gonna call you a kiss ass or a pussy and they're gonna take advantage of you. Next time I bust your balls, I want you to stand up to me. I'm gonna give you shit for bein' late cuz that's my job, but I know you ain't usually late! So gimme shit right back! Don't you get it? A man's gotta right to rant and rave, but if I really have a problem with you we'll be havin' a private conversation."

"So you want me to argue with you?" I asked, totally confused. That was the kind of thing that would get me backhanded by my dad. I spent my whole life learning how to defuse an angry man and now I was being told to do the opposite.

"Hell yeah! I mean, don't be late again, but if you are, stand up to me. Tell me you ain't usually late, give me hell right back. It's just what guys do. Now if you're late all the time, we're gonna have a problem, but that's different."

"Okay, Don, I'll try."

"No, Ray. Don't try. Do. Save that sweet talk for your girlfriend."

I almost said, "Yes sir," out of habit and caught myself just in time. "Alright then, can I get back to work?"

"Yeah, you're on paint duty today, and remember -"

I cut him off, "This ain't the gawd damned Tawj Mahawl," I said, using my best New York accent.

I was really glad to be painting because I could do it alone, see my progress, and think. There was so much on my mind that my thoughts were bumping into each other. Frustration, anxiety, and bliss were all fighting for dominance. I tried to reminisce about my night and even my morning with Alicia. She looked so sexy sitting on her kitchen counter in her tank top and panties. Damn, she looked good this morning!

And then there was the matter of her telling me she overeats and throws up. In a way, it made me feel a lot closer to her, like she wasn't perfect – she was vulnerable – but I worried that she'd keep doing it. Then there was being late and getting bitched out and being told to man up. I thought about that a lot. I didn't really know if I wanted to be in charge of other guys. Maybe I'd rather just paint with my headphones on. Then I thought about

Alicia some more, about how sweet and sexy she is and how I can't wait to see her again. Then I worried about the new guys not respecting me.

I decided to listen to some music and drown out my thoughts. I put on some of the new music that Alicia had put on my phone. Most of it was stuff I picked out, some R & B, and I got in the groove of painting. Then one of those hillbilly songs came on and I practiced restraint by not pressing the "next" button. The music was really fast and I noticed I picked up the pace of my painting, a lot actually. The music reminded me of a movie on fast forward and I was really moving quickly without that slow bass beat I was used to. I'd have to tell Alicia I found her music useful. I wanted to call her, but knew she was at work by now and I'm not supposed to be on the phone either.

Lenny came back to the apartment carrying a new sink for the bathroom and said, "Good, you're almost done. We can get this sink in today and be done here. So how come you was late? You party too hard last night?"

"Naw, man, that's not it. I kinda got into something with my girlfriend this morning."

"Well, the way you've been grinnin', you must have had some good make-up sex."

I didn't answer and tried to stop grinning. Lenny shook his head and he held the sink in place while I hooked it up. I went back to painting and was all done by four and the guys were already gone to the new jobsite. I called Don and told him I finished and he said to lock up the place and gave me an address where I could meet him tomorrow. Finally, I could talk to Alicia.

I sat outside on the building's stoop and texted her, "Hey Dream-Girl, can you talk?"

I waited for a few minutes until she texted back, "I've been thinking about you all day! I'm outside my professor's office. I'll call you as soon as I'm out."

It seemed even hotter than it did at noon, the air was so still and full of humidity. The pedestrian traffic seemed to be on a slower speed and everyone looked irritated. I was a little bit concerned about how Alicia did on her test and why she was talking to her professor, but the first part of her text said she was thinking about me too. I joined the slow parade, but zipped through them quickly and strategically so I could get home and shower. At home I did a series of push ups and sit ups, then ate three peanut butter and jelly sandwiches before hopping into the shower. I was sitting down with a book when my phone finally rang.

"Hey," I said. "How are you? Is everything okay?"

"Well, yes and no," Alicia answered. "I got my test back today and I got a 92."

"Oh, that's good, right? An A?"

"Well, not really. Remember I got a B last time and I needed to get a 95 to keep my A in the class. I went and met with my professor to see what I need to do and if there is any extra credit or anything."

"And?"

"He doesn't give any extra credit and now I need a 97 on the final. That's nearly impossible, Ray, but he gave me some good tips on what to focus on for the final exam, so I'm glad I talked to him."

"Dang, a 97? That's a lot of pressure." I felt myself tensing up.

"I know. But I can do it. I have to do it. How was your day? Were you late?"

"Yeah, and my boss gave me shit, which I expected, but the funny thing is he then gave me shit for not standing up to him."

"Really?"

"Yeah. I guess I need to learn how guys interact in the construction world. I'm only used to working with my dad, and then at my last job, we worked in this office building and the boss was a really mellow guy and, I don't know... Don's talking about putting me in charge of some new guys."

"Wow, really? That's great! You just barely started there and you're already getting a promotion?"

"Yeah, I guess you could call it that, but it isn't because I'm that anything special. He got really busy and doesn't have any choice. I don't know if he has much faith in me and I'm not so sure I do either."

"Yes, but he has a lot of experience and must know what he's doing. I'm sure he could hire a supervisor if he didn't see something in you. I'm really proud of you, Ray."

"Really?" That felt like the nicest thing she could say to me. I was dying to crawl through the phone and kiss her right then so I said, "I wish I was there right now. I'd kiss your pretty mouth and throw you down on that futon."

"I'd like that," she giggled. "I've been thinking about you all day! My coworker teased me for smiling so much."

"Really? I got busted for smiling too."

"Aww, when do I get to see you again?"

"Well, you tell me. You're the busy girl. I'm free and easy."

Alicia laughed and said, "Well, it is already kind of late and I am going to need to study tonight, but tomorrow I am meeting my study group after work at the library. I was kind of hoping you could meet me there and ride the subway home with me and maybe stay at my place if you wanted?"

"Can we get some Pho on the way to the subway again?"

"Oh my god, you are the best," she laughed. "But, Ray, I'm going to have to *study* at the library!" She emphasized the word "study" and went on, "And you'll get to meet my group. But we won't be done until about seven or seven-thirty."

"That works for me. I'm going to let you go study right now, Dream-Girl."

"Okay, one more thing. I did look up the yellow and red rose. Do you know what that really means?"

"Yes I do."

"I was hoping so," she said, and paused for a few seconds. "Goodnight, Ray. Dream about me, okay?"

I laughed and told her I dream about her all day long, and said goodnight.

The next day, Don gave us our new "DT Construction" t-shirts. He met me at the loft-conversion site and I was excited to see it. The building had seven floors with these old metal-framed windows with cranks on them that went from the floor to the ceiling. Don said it had brick walls we were going to uncover, but right now they were buried under drywall. The first thing he wanted to do was clear out the second floor. It used to be a clothing factory and there were all these old industrial sewing machines that we needed to take apart and then scrap the metal, which meant take it to a recycling facility. He said a delivery was coming and he wanted to leave me there so I could sign for the materials. I could start working on the machines and piling the parts next to the door while I waited. Lenny and I could load them in the truck later.

Then Don handed me my first paycheck. It had not calculated what I would make in a week because I wasn't sure what the taxes would be, but it seemed pretty good. Now that I had a general idea, I needed to calculate how much it would be per month and figure out if I can afford to stay in my apartment alone. If I need a roommate, I would move into someone else's place with a private room. I also needed to open a bank account so I could quit giving the check cashing place part of my money. I folded my paycheck up and put it in my wallet and said out loud, "Congratulations, Joe-citizen."

I spent hours working alone, listening to music, disassembling the sewing machines and building up the pile of parts. Two guys came with a big delivery of boxes: wood, drywall, and pvc pipe. I told them to put it all on the first floor in the space Don had shown me. Then I counted the materials and signed their paperwork. They were missing one pallet, so I told the guys and they wrote "back order" and initialed it, then gave me a copy. I texted Don to let him know that everything arrived and one thing was back ordered, and he told me to keep working on clearing the factory floor as long as I wanted. I didn't want to seem like I wanted to leave early so I stayed one hour late and got a ton of work done, then I took the subway home for a quick shower, made some peanut butter sandwiches to eat on the go, and headed over to the library to meet Alicia.

She had texted me earlier to say they decided to meet at the St. Agnes branch, which was good news only because it was closer to both our apartments and I could walk there. It has a bunch of little side rooms with glass walls for groups to meet in and I knew she'd be in one of those. I did see Alicia in a room with two guys and two other girls and a bunch of books and papers spread out on a table. I didn't know if I should interrupt, so I texted her, but she didn't answer. I tried walking by the room twice, but she didn't seem to notice me. I positioned myself off to the side where she (and maybe one of the girls) could see me and started doing a funny dance. Alicia still didn't notice me, but some lady in the library commented, "Nice moves" as she walked by.

I decided to just sit down with a book where she would see me if she came out. I got into reading, and after a short while felt hands on my shoulders from behind and looked up to see Alicia's pretty face. "I saw your sexy dance. It was so hard not to laugh."

"You think my dancing is funny?" I reached up and pulled her head in for a kiss.

"Um, no, I actually could tell you are a mighty fine dancer, but I think yours skills should be observed outside of a library."

"You should see me salsa."

"Oh my god, you can salsa dance?"

"I'm Puerto Rican! You don't think my mom would leave this earth without making sure her boy can salsa, do you?"

"I want you to teach me! Tonight! Lessons start at my place, as soon as we finish this chapter we are on."

Damn. She obviously wasn't done studying. "How much longer?"

"We aren't even close to done, but the library closes at seven. I told my group I had to go to the bathroom, but I better get back in there." It was 6:40 p.m. and I was happy to hang out and read.

I was in line at the counter to check out the book I had started when I saw Alicia's group emerge from the study room. When they approached, Alicia introduced me to Monica, Caleb, Brianna, and Joey, and I shook hands with the guys. The group seemed friendly enough, but Monica looked me up and down and said, "So, you work construction?" I thought I saw a slight roll of her eyes. She was a pretty Asian girl holding a stack of books in front of her chest. I answered, "Yes," and she said, "Hmmm," gave a slight shoulder shrug, and started looking at her phone.

She and the others said good bye and Alicia got in line with me. "What are you getting?" she asked, eyeing the book in my hand.

"It's called *The Power of the Dog* and it's really good. I decided to take a break from Manhattan and head out west," I said in a cowboy voice. Alicia giggled and took my hand.

We walked back to Alicia's place through the thick fog of humidity. I insisted on carrying Alicia's book bag and she made too big of a deal about it, going on about what a gentleman I was, but really, I was just thinking about how if I notice a couple walking and she is carrying something and he isn't, I always assume the guy is a complete ass.

By the time we got to her place, we both were covered in sweat with wet spots down the back of our shirts. Alicia said she wanted to take a shower and asked with a demure grin if I wanted to join her. Hell yeah, I did. The first thought that crossed my mind was: *I am going to be showering with my sexy Dream-Girl!* The second thought? *Wow, two showers in one day!* In the past year I often went weeks without a shower. Now I was about to get in the shower

148

with Alicia. I sure would not have predicted either of these events just a few weeks ago. It was impossible to contain my excitement, which made her giggle as we both shed our clothes in her ultra-feminine bathroom.

She turned on the water and tested it with her hand, then stepped into the shower and held out her hand for me to join her. As soon as I did, we embraced and began kissing, not even bothering to pretend that cleaning up was our priority.

With the warm water running down my skin and Alicia wrapped in my arms, I was in sensory overload-heaven. Water was cascading down our bodies and even entering our mouths as we intermittently opened them for kisses. My hands roamed her backside and she pushed me back slightly and picked up a plastic bottle of very sweet smelling soap. She poured some onto my chest with a smile on her face, then set the bottle down and began using her hands to spread the soap all over me, which made it bubble and foam. I pressed into her and covered her body with soapy foam as well so that I could have my turn rubbing the soap all over her sexy wet body. I paid particular attention to her chest.

"I'm pretty sure I have the cleanest tits in New York City right now," she laughed, and I answered, "Let me make sure you have the cleanest butt to match." I squeezed some soap onto my hands and rubbed them together before massaging her lower back and butt with the soap, enjoying the slippery feeling as my hands glided easily over her skin. Alicia was rubbing her chest into mine as I soaped her entire back and bottom, and then I slipped a hand to the front and between her legs. She gasped and then gently bit my shoulder, as she lifted one leg to give me better access. She put her foot on the soap dish and I held onto her firmly with one arm around her waist so she wouldn't slip, as I slid a finger into her and curled it. "Mmmmm," she moaned, "Condoms?"

"Yes, but not yet," I answered. I felt no urgency to rush

things along. I wanted to enjoy the wet smoothness of our soapy bodies rubbing together, and the warm flow of the water streaming around us. Alicia dropped her soapy hand down to grasp my hardness and made double-sure that we were, in fact, the cleanest couple in all of Manhattan. Now I was losing my patience and wanted to enter her in the shower, so I told her to stay put while I stepped out to retrieve a condom from my pants lying on the bathroom floor.

When I stepped back in, Alicia took the condom out of my hand, tore open the package, and rolled the condom onto me. She was pretty good at that, I thought. Then I winced at the awareness that she had done this before, but caught my negative spiral before it slipped too far. She is twenty-four and I should be glad that she knows how to use a condom. At that very moment she turned around and rubbed her sweet bottom into me, and there was no room in my mind for bad thoughts. I was overwhelmed when she presented herself in this position, her butt against my groin and her whole front side exposed for my hands to roam.

I entered her from behind as Alicia bent slightly to accommodate me. She planted one foot back on the soap dish and held herself steady with one hand on the wall. I placed my hands on both of her hips and kissed her shoulder as we moved in rhythm together. Alicia lifted her free hand and brought it to the side of my neck. As a result, her back arched, her foot slipped, and she almost fell, but I steadied her and we both laughed in relief. "Would you mind terribly if we moved to the futon?" she asked, and of course I didn't mind. We each grabbed a towel, and wrapping them around ourselves, not really taking the time to dry, we practically ran to the futon. Alicia laid her towel down, and then laid her wet body down on top of it.

I smiled and paused to admire her beautiful body. She had her knees bent and I couldn't resist burying my face between her squeaky clean legs, which caused her to squeal, but I didn't spend much time there. I kissed my way up to her mouth and slid back into her sweetness from the front side. Alicia drew me close and planted her lips at my ear, where she began whispering, telling me how much she liked what I was doing. She wrapped her legs around me and was moaning my name softly as I made love to her as gently and slowly as my current mood demanded, until she became more aggressive. I could feel her fingernails digging into my butt cheeks and I didn't mind at all, as she also started bucking her hips. This required a different tempo that I could not possibly sustain for long, but didn't need to as she murmured the obvious in my ear; that she had reached her climax, sending me over the crest of my own until I collapsed on top of her.

I raised myself up on my elbows to kiss her when she requested – or almost demanded – "Ray, teach me to salsa dance!"

"Right now?" I laughed. I thought girls always wanted to cuddle right after.

"Yes, please, right now!" was her answer.

And so we got up and put our underwear back on and Alicia also put on a tank top while I found some salsa music on the computer. I demonstrated the basic steps, and then held her in my arms while we practiced the "quick, quick, slow" dance step. Alicia caught on quickly and I was able to teach her the basic turn and even the cross body lead. Alicia mastered all the technicalities just fine, but she didn't have any pizzazz to her movement.

I was trying to think of a nice way to tell her she was dancing like a white girl and I realized this was a job for Sha-Nay-Nay. Sure, Sha-Nay-Nay is a strong black woman and not a Puerto Rican salsa dancer, but she could sure teach Alicia a thing about "shakin' that booty" and so I said, "Girl, lemme show you how to put some spice in your step," and demonstrated this thing my mom would do with her hips at the end of each turn.

I must have looked pretty funny salsa dancing like a girl in nothing but my boxer shorts because Alicia was cracking up. I showed her another move where the girl drags her hand over her head after a cross over turn and it looks really sexy when girls do it, but I am sure I looked pretty silly. I got Alicia to try it but she was still being kind of stiff and reserved and shy.

Sha-Nay-Nay encouraged her, but begged for more because you really need to exaggerate these moves in salsa. I don't think Alicia knew how extreme was acceptable in salsa dancing, so I danced like a woman for my girlfriend and after a few minutes, I had Alicia laughing and copying my exaggerated hip swings, which was completely appropriate and utterly sexy. I went back to my normal voice to tell her so.

"You got it, baby. I want to take you out dancing."

"Really?" She asked, smiling at me and very happy with herself.

"Yes. Saturday night. I want to take you salsa dancing."

"Oh my god, you are the best boyfriend ever." Alicia turned off the music and hugged me.

Her comment stunned me for a second. I didn't ever think about it or try to be a good boyfriend; I'm just crazy about Alicia and want to do things with her. If I'm good it's because she brings it out in me. And so I told her, "I'm not that great. But you make me want to be a better person."

"I can't see how you need to be any better. You are like the kindest, funniest, sweetest person I know." She turned to her keyboard and said, "But you do need to be on time for work tomorrow. What time should I set my alarm?"

"Six-thirty should be okay." I didn't really know how to

respond to those compliments so I started kissing her shoulders.

Alicia grinned at me and asked, "Does six-thirty allow enough time for wake-up sex?"

I laughed at that and said, "Set the alarm back an extra half hour, Dream-Girl," and I kissed her goodnight and dreamt about salsa dancing with my girl.

10 - CORN

I was having the best dream ever: Alicia was going down on me, actually licking me, as I petted her soft hair. Then as I grew hard she took me in her mouth, and as I slowly became conscious I realized I wasn't dreaming at all! "Mmmmm," I greeted her, "What a nice way to wake up. I thought I was dreaming at first. No wonder I call you Dream-Girl." Alicia giggled and crawled on top of me and kissed me right by my ear.

"Good morning," she whispered.

"Mmmmhmmm, yes, it is."

Alicia clambered over me to grab a condom out of the desk drawer that was right next to the futon. Her position put her tits right in my face, so I did what came naturally as my hands found their way to her ass. We now had condoms stashed in each of the three rooms of her tiny apartment, always just a few steps away. Alicia tore the foil wrapper open and began rolling the condom onto me. "Hey," I said, "don't I get to play with you for a while first?"

"Not this time!" she answered. "We can't let you be late to work. Especially now that you are an important supervisor." And then she straddled me and lowered herself smoothly onto my very willing member.

"Whoa, I am still coming out of a dream state. How'd you get so ready?"

"Waking up next to you does that to me." Alicia grinned as she began riding me slowly. I was overcome with tenderness for her. I could not believe how lucky I was to have this amazing girl so crazy about me. Her hair was all wild in the morning and she looked incredibly beautiful, so I told her, "Have I ever told you how beautiful you are?"

"Yes, but I'll never get tired of hearing it," she smiled at me. I just enjoyed watching her as she took complete control, so confident and so sexy. I kept thinking "Wow, I am so damn lucky."

Alicia lowered her body onto mine and was grinding into me and I felt what she was trying to do, how she was attempting to rub herself, so I pulled her hips down even farther creating an indescribable friction. I felt her body flush with sweat and it was so sexy to see and feel these bodily changes come over her. I could have cum right at that second, except I was lucky to have had so much sex lately that I had a natural restraint. I waited until I was sure she was going to climax before releasing my own orgasm. Alicia lay panting on me and covered in sweat and I thought it was the greatest feeling ever, to have this hot sticky babe on top of me, but she got all self-conscious about it and jumped up to take a shower. I washed myself off at the sink because I shower after work and, well, honestly... I wasn't that eager to get the smell of her off of me. I kind of like it – hell, I downright love it.

I looked in her fridge for anything to eat, but it was empty, so I knocked on the bathroom door and told her I had to get to work. She opened the door and had a towel on her head and kissed me good bye. "Thank you," she said.

"For what?"

"For the good-morning sex," she smiled at me.

That made me laugh. "Alicia, you really are my Dream-Girl. You know that?"

"I hope so."

And I hauled ass to work and made it ten minutes early, wearing a ridiculous grin I could not wipe off my face even if I tried. I got there before either Don or Lenny showed up. When he did arrive, Don gave me instructions for the day and he and Lenny both stayed and worked at the loft too. I am not sure what they were doing, but I was ripping down dry wall, which was kind of a nasty job, but it was cool to see the old brick underneath.

At lunchtime I checked my phone and saw a text that had come from Alicia that morning that said, "I had so much fun last night!" I texted back, "Showering or salsa lessons?" I was thinking both. And then I thought about our morning quickie and kissing her goodbye while she had that towel on her head. I was feeling more comfortable with her now and definitely more comfortable within myself.

We didn't make plans to see each other that night, but I knew that on Friday I was going to hang out with her at her apartment. We would have one more practice session before I took her out salsa dancing on Saturday night. Today I just planned to go home and take a shower and head over to the library. When I got home, I opened the door and jumped two feet in the air when I saw a guy sitting on my futon. *Thomas!*

"Damn, man. I wasn't expecting you!" My mind quickly processed the fact that Thomas still had a key. *Dammit, why hadn't I changed the lock?* Then there was the matter of him actually paying his part of the rent. *Did I need to let him stay?*

"Hey, I'm sorry, man. I woulda' called first, but I realized I don't even have your number! I hope you don't mind I let myself in. At first I thought I was in the wrong apartment!" He held his arms out gesturing to how different everything looked. He looked like he had filled out and had a completely different demeanor, not like the Thomas I remembered at all.

"So what do you want?" I asked, rather coldly. After the bitch-out session I got from Don when he accused me of being too nice, I had been thinking about my situation with my roommates and knew I would never let myself get in a predicament like that again. I noticed he had his key and an envelope on the coffee table and a big shopping bag on the floor.

"I came to say good bye, for one thing. I'm going to Arizona to stay in a program. I got fifteen days clean." He was smiling and holding his hands out in a "look at me" gesture, but I still didn't trust him. "But also, I need to talk to you about some stuff." He suddenly seemed nervous and I wasn't cutting him any slack; I was still standing, he was still sitting, and I was staring him down.

"Well, man, Ray, man... I treated you real bad." He looked at me and I still felt I didn't recognize him. "I was really messed up, man, and I know I was like the worst person to live with in the world. Not to mention..." Thomas paused and looked around. "Well, just look at this place. It looks good now, man, it really does."

I maintained my silence, which in this case did not feel passive. I was kind of enjoying seeing him squirm.

"Well, I just wanted to say, well... I know sorry doesn't cut it. I took a bunch of your stuff and I want to make it right. I'm not going to stay, but I brought you the rent and a thirty-day notice."

"You're giving me a formal notice and paying the rent but not staying?" I laughed as I added, "Un-fucking-believable."

"Yeah, man, it's the right thing to do. Well, the truth is my mom's been paying my rent anyway, but when I talked to my sponsor, he said I need to make things right with you and I will pay my mom back over time – hell, I owe that woman a lot – but anyway, yeah...."

"What's a sponsor?"

"A guy that's helping me work my steps. I'm in a twelve-step program and I am on my ninth step." He sat up straighter and was smiling now. I didn't feel familiar with this version of Thomas and I still didn't know if I could trust this one any more than the old one. He could be up to something.

"What's in the bag?" I asked.

His posture shrank as Thomas answered, "Clothes. I brought you some clothes. I took a lot of your stuff, Ray. I wish I could just give you a check – and I do plan to send you some money once I start working – but in the meantime I brought you some of my clothes I had at my mom's house."

"I don't want your damn clothes."

Thomas cringed like I had smacked him. *This guy who harassed me for months was suddenly all sensitive.* "I don't blame you, but they're not just old clothes I don't want. I brought you some good stuff, but honestly, most of it is warm clothes I won't need in Arizona."

"I'll give it to the homeless."

"Well, it's yours to do whatever you want with. Listen, man, I'm sorry. I don't know what else to say, except I intend to send you money once I get settled for all the stuff I took, your books, that toaster, your iPod, shoes –"

"Forget about it," I waved my hand in the air. I was getting pissed hearing this itemized list of all my missing stuff, "Good luck in Arizona. I am glad you came by and paid the rent. That was pretty decent of you."

Thomas stood and shook my hand, "Any idea what happened to Jeff?" I told him the story about how Jeff tried to kick the door in and the cops took him away and said he mugged a lady and stole her purse. Thomas got all teary-eyed, which surprised me, and he put his hand on his chest and said, "That could've been me, man. Jeff and me, we were doing the same shit, but now he's in jail and I got fifteen days clean! What does that tell you?"

"That you got the better deal."

"I sure did, Ray," his voice cracked and he walked out the door shaking his head, "I sure did get the better deal."

I locked the door behind him and stood there shaking my head at what an unexpected visit that was. I decided to take a luxurious shower before heading over to the Mid-Manhattan library. I dumped out the contents of the bag Thomas had left and was pleasantly surprised. There were two decent pairs of jeans and a pair of running shoes that looked almost new, plus a few button-up shirts. There were also a few warm clothes I put in the closet, and then I took the whole bag with me as well as my new work shirts to give to Louisa for washing.

"Look at you, high roller now?" Louisa teased me as I handed her the bag of clothes and pre-paid with a ten-dollar bill.

"I'm a working man now," I laughed, and asked "Hey, can

you wash my work shirts separate? I don't know if the jeans will fade on them."

"I wash everything separate, don't you know that?" Louisa asked. Funny, it never even occurred to me how she washed my clothes, but she held her door open further so I could see inside. She had a small apartment like mine with clotheslines strung across the room and a bunch of clothes hanging drying right there in her apartment. I couldn't see any place to sit and I couldn't suppress a "Whoa" as I got a glimpse of her living conditions. It made me kind of sad.

"I wash all the clothes by hand in the bathtub, hang them up to dry, and iron them."

"Wow!" I didn't know what else to say. "You should charge more."

"Oh yeah? Well maybe I do, you ever think of that?"

"Really?"

Louisa leaned in and whispered, "Depends on if I like the person. You got the best rate, but now that you're workin' your prices went up." And then I spontaneously hugged her and startled us both.

I didn't see William at the library and I was kind of glad because I didn't really want to talk books today. Instead, I was using one of the free computers to find a place where Alicia and I could go salsa dancing. I found one that Carlos and I had gone to a few times that I couldn't remember the location of, then I did a search to see if I could find a good Puerto Rican restaurant to take Alicia to. Casa Adela looked perfect and was right up the street from the dance club, but then I wondered if Alicia would eat that kind of food. It got me thinking, so I Googled eating disorders.

I didn't like what I was reading. In fact, it was scaring me and depressing me, but then I remembered that the internet was probably giving me the worst-case scenario.

"Wonderful." I looked up and saw William standing over me. I saw his eyes glance at the screen. "I've been replaced by a digital apparatus with no intrinsic capacity for discernment?"

"Oh, hey man. Naw, man, not looking for a book, just using the internet."

William paused and looked from me to the screen, "Is this about that pretty blonde, Allison?"

"Alicia."

William pulled up a chair and sat down. "How deep are you?" he asked.

"What do you mean?"

"I mean how into this girl are you?"

"Deep," I admitted.

William dragged his hand across the top of his head and took a deep breath. He had a very concerned look on his face that wasn't making me feel any better, "Well, Ray, I don't know if you have any experience with this, but..." He paused.

"What?"

"It's really just the tip of the iceberg, usually."

I got the feeling William knew what he was talking about and probably not just from reading. "You know how it is, don't you?"

"Unfortunately, yes. My sister..." William trailed off.

"Is she okay now?"

"I don't think she'll ever be completely okay, but she's a lot better now. Put our parents through hell, then her poor husband..."

"She's married?" I got hopeful, thinking she must be doing pretty well.

"Yes, she's a mom too, but she had a really really hard time getting pregnant. It took years and the emotional toll was immense."

It sounded to me like everything worked out okay. Besides, I didn't think Alicia seemed that bad off. She must only have a mild case, so I told William so and he laughed.

"Well, I hope you're right. For your sake too. It's tough loving someone who hurts herself."

I sat in silence knowing he was right, but wasn't there something I could I do? "Is there any way I can help her?" I asked.

"There are lots of ways to be helpful to her. There are a few ways you could probably make it worse. But ultimately it is up to her. You can't fix this, Ray." William shook his head slowly and thoughtfully. I felt myself sinking and didn't know what to say.

I nodded and sat thinking. Who knew William could be so normal and such a bum-out at the same time? But then he snapped out of it. All of a sudden he perked up and reasserted his theatrical style as he said, "My day here is done and I'm famished! I am about to dine at a quaint little Vietnamese establishment that serves divine noodles, would you care to join me?"

"Pho?" I laughed, "Sure, I'm in." It felt really good to have a little money in my pocket and to be able to just say "yes" to an invite, but I was also relieved that Pho is cheap. I wouldn't want to waste money dining with William when I have a beautiful girlfriend to take on dates. That reminded me, "I'm gonna go call Alicia real quick and meet you out front."

William went wherever he goes when not in the public eye and I tried calling Alicia, but she didn't answer. I had not heard from her since that early text, but that didn't surprise me since I knew she was studying with her group. I texted her, "Hey beautiful. I'm going to eat Pho with William. Don't be jealous." I meant about the Pho, but I was teasing her about liking William. I also missed her so I added a second text saying just that.

By the time I got off the subway and walked home, it was after ten o'clock and I still had not heard from Alicia. It was weird that she had not at least sent a text, but I tried not to trip on it. There were many possible reasons: she could have fallen asleep, let her phone battery die... I tried not to think about it and just go to bed, but I didn't sleep well.

When I woke after a fitful night, I checked my phone first thing and saw a text, but it was from Don telling me what to do at work and that he'd be in later. I texted Alicia again, hoping I wasn't overdoing it, but I was really surprised I had not heard from her yet. My text said, "I will call at lunch. Miss you." I hoped for one of those texts back saying she was busy but missed me too with some of those corny little hearts, but it didn't come.

By lunchtime I really was worried. I called her again, but didn't leave a message. Maybe she had lost her phone? Maybe she wasn't getting texts? I decided to leave a message, "Hey babe, call me when you can." I put my phone on vibrate in my pocket and planned to answer if it rang. I even warned Don that I might get a quick phone call, some important business I needed to handle, and he said, "No problem, just don't make a habit out of it," but my phone never buzzed.

When the longest day of my life finally ended, I knew I wasn't going home. I practically ran to Alicia's apartment to see if she was there. I rang the intercom and didn't get an answer. Then I noticed a piece of paper taped to the intercom. It said "Ray" on the outside and if I hadn't been in such a hurry I would have noticed it before ringing. I snatched it and opened and read, "Alicia doesn't have her phone, you can reach her through me." I was signed, Janice – Alicia's mom – and had a phone number.

This didn't make any sense. Alicia hadn't said her mom was coming from California. That would be a pretty big deal and I think she would have said something, wouldn't she? And why would she leave me a note? There was no time to waste, and I called the number on the paper. She didn't answer, so I left a message pleading with her to call me. I didn't know what to do with myself, if I should go home or wait there or what, so I just started pacing around checking my phone every thirty seconds. I finally made up my mind to walk toward my apartment and that's when my phone rang. It was her mom's number but Alicia's voice asking, "Ray? Did you get the note?" She sounded panicky.

"Yes of course. Tell me, are you okay?"

"Well, yes, sort of. I'm sorry, Ray, I... well, something happened and I didn't have a chance to get my purse or my phone out of my desk drawer at work and oh my god, I didn't even know how to get ahold of you so I made my mom leave that note, and hey there is no Raymond Kelly listed, you know, I sent you a facebook message this morning and..."

"Alicia, where are you? What happened?"

"I'm in the hospital," she whispered. "But I'm okay, don't

worry."

"What hospital?"

"Lenox."

"I'm coming down there," I answered, so relieved to hear her voice.

"Wait, Ray, listen, before you do I want to tell you what happened because my mom is not in the room right now and, well, you are going to have to meet her and she's really upset about this and making a huge deal about it when really it isn't..."

I cut her off, "What happened?"

"Well," she whispered, "I fainted at work and someone called 911 and, well, they said I was having a heart attack, but really it was just that my electrolytes were all messed up and I think they just have to take you in when that happens and..."

"A heart attack?" I yelled into the phone.

"Well, yes, that is what they call it but it is really mild, Ray, not like when..."

"I'm on my way." I hung up and started running for the subway station. I was shaking and angry and pumped full of adrenaline. I don't know exactly why I was angry, except my twenty-four-year-old girlfriend just informed me that she had a heart attack, but was acting like it was no big deal and for some reason that really pissed me off. But I wanted to be with her as soon as possible and see for myself if she was really okay.

I realized the hospital was not that far, but it would take two subways to get there, so I flagged down a taxi and told him to get me to Lenox Hill Hospital. I swear I could have run there faster, there was so much adrenaline surging through me. My mind was racing, going crazy wondering how the hell Alicia could have a heart attack. I asked the cab driver, "You ever hear of a young girl having a heart attack?"

"Yeah, if they have a heart condition or if they're on amphetamines," was his answer. I wished I hadn't asked.

He got me to the hospital and I paid him and jumped out and asked the lady at the front desk where I could find Alica Klaer. She gave me a room number and I skipped the elevator and ran up the stairs. When I walked towards the room I saw a woman on her cell phone who was obviously Alicia's mom and I saw her look at me and say, "I'll call you back." I didn't pause. I walked straight into the room and there she was, Alicia sitting up in bed looking completely normal except for the hospital gown and the IV tube in her arm. I hugged her and held her and heaved a sigh of relief.

"I'm sorry. I didn't mean to scare you."

I didn't answer. I just looked at her and touched her cheek and kissed her on the lips and scooted back on the bed to look at her. She was smiling but looking apologetic at the same time, and I asked, "Tell me what happened."

"I'd better tell you." I turned around and saw Alicia's mom standing in the room. "I'm Janice, Alicia's mom, and you must be Ray."

I stood and took her outstretched hand and she said, "I hoped to meet you under better circumstances. I flew out last night when I got the call. Sorry we couldn't get in touch with you. Alicia thought you might be worried."

"Yeah, I was," I admitted, thinking that was an understatement. I looked back at Alicia and she had her arms folded across her chest and a rather pissed-off look on her face, but she was staring at the wall. I could see that she didn't want her mom's version of what happened get to me first.

"Do you mind if we step outside? Alicia really doesn't need any more stress right now."

"No, Mom, you can just talk in front of me. Besides, I told you Ray already knows," Alicia argued.

Janice stared at Alicia for a few seconds before saying, "Then you won't mind if I talk to him for a minute. He can hear your version too, but I've come all this way and I think Ray would be interested in knowing why."

"Fine. Just give us a moment of privacy first, please," Alicia retorted in a tone I had never before heard from her.

Her mom said fine, she was going to make a phone call, and she stepped out.

"What's going on?" I asked. I was sitting on the side of the bed holding Alicia's hand. She continued looking at the wall instead of at me and said, "My mom is obviously very upset and she is making a really big deal about this. I guess I can't blame her. It must have been pretty scary when the hospital called, but... I don't want her to get you all upset or paint me out to be a psycho or anything."

"This is because of your eating disorder, right?"

Alicia looked at me briefly, then away, then back at me and said, "Yes." Her eyes were full of tears. "I know she's going to tell you bad things about me, Ray. I'm really scared."

"Why would your mom say bad things about you?"

Alicia paused before saying, "She's worried about me. She's pretty upset right now. Please just keep that in mind, okay?" She squeezed my hand and pleaded with urgency, "And please don't leave after you talk to her!"

"I won't," I promised. I lifted her hand to my mouth and kissed it and said, "I am so glad you are okay. That was the second worst phone call I ever got in my life."

"What was the worst?"

"To come home, that my mom was at the end. I kept thinking she was going to pull through and get better. I should have known, but I didn't."

Alicia squeezed my hand again and said, "I'm going to be okay. I promise." And then I heard Janice clear her throat, so I stood and kissed Alicia on the cheek and walked out of the room. Janice asked if we could go down to the cafeteria because she wanted coffee and I agreed.

We both got coffee and sat down at a table. Janice looked to be around fifty and attractive, but more cute than pretty. She had Alicia's coloring, and a little upturned nose and bouncy hairdo that made her look young. But she wore a pained expression with a downturned mouth and her eyes looked like she had been crying instead of sleeping. I too wished I was meeting her under better circumstances.

"So, Alicia told you about her bulimia?" I nodded and she went on, "But I am confident she downplayed it and it is impossible for you to know the severity of the problem." She looked at me and I didn't know what the right response was. It wasn't really a question.

I guess she took that as a sign to go on.

"I got the horrifying call yesterday that she had a heart attack, but was told she was stable and going to be okay. I got on the first flight out here. My husband is caring for our other daughters, but he will fly out next weekend and then I'll fly home."

"Why did she have a heart attack?" I asked.

"Electrolyte imbalance, low potassium, the stress probably didn't help, but the cardiologist said the low potassium was the main factor and was directly caused by dehydration and excessive vomiting. Alicia is right when she says it was a mild heart attack, but her making light of this situation just infuriates me. It is an indication of how sick she still is."

I didn't argue with that, I knew she was right. I put my head in my hands and rubbed my forehead, feeling really stressed and depressed.

"This must be hard on you, Ray. I'm sorry. You're new to this and I've been dealing with it for many years. That is why I may seem harsh. I'm really frustrated and scared for my daughter." Her voice sounded normal and steady but tears were running down her face.

I put my hand out and rested it on hers. I had no words.

She went on, "We thought she was doing okay. She told us she was, but..." She sat silently crying and wiping her tears with those hard paper napkins.

"Can't she get help for this?" I asked naively and Janice almost snorted, "Two outpatient programs, one residential, plus years and years of therapy. I've tried things you can't even imagine. I'm really at my wits' end."

"Why does she do it?"

"That's a good question and obviously there is no simple answer, but one factor is Alicia puts too much pressure on herself, more than she can sustain, and then she breaks down. Then she pulls herself together and repeats the cycle all over again. We didn't want her to move out here, you know."

"I didn't know that."

"Her father and I don't put this pressure on her. She does this to herself; she always has. Even before the eating, when she was just a little girl, she used to impose all these rules on herself and we used to think it was cute and funny and call her "Little Miss Perfect" – god, I wish we hadn't; I wish we would have seen the path she was on, and..."

"You shouldn't blame yourself. I have been reading about this recently and it sounds like you have done everything you could."

"Yes," she nodded. Then she straightened herself up and said, "Well... yes. And we are not giving up. I'll never give up on my little girl."

I removed my hand from hers and swallowed my last bit of coffee and asked, "I hope you don't mind. I want to go talk to her."

"No, go talk to her. I'm going to stay here and make a few phone calls." She wiped her face and smoothed her hair and gave me a forced smile.

I walked slowly back up to Alicia's room, feeling like my legs were made of lead. I didn't know what I could possibly say to her, but I just wanted to be with her. When I walked into the room she looked at me with a worried expression. I must have looked pretty beat and it occurred to me that she had seen that expression from her family and other people that have cared about her. I sat on the side of the bed and tried not to look too bummed out.

"I'm sorry," she whispered in a tiny voice. "I'm really sorry to scare you and my family. I thought I was doing okay because I was using markers this time."

"Markers?"

"Corn," she said. She was twisting the sheet in her hand and kept looking at her hands then back at me. She went on in a soft voice, "I was using corn as a marker. I would eat a small healthy meal and then when I was done I would eat some corn, so then when I overate and threw up I would know when the corn came up it was time to stop and leave the healthy meal in my system."

I stared at her stunned. I felt like I was watching a tsunami bearing down on us. The sudden awareness of how deeply sick she was and how unaware she was of the danger to herself made me feel lost, swallowed up, at a total loss of control. I felt like I wanted to yell "Run!" and save her from the danger, but she was standing with her back to the tsunami unable to hear me. My frustration felt like a punch in the gut and my anxiety was so great I didn't know what to do with myself, so I stood up and walked out so she wouldn't see me get emotional. I walked quickly outside and did a bunch of math problems in my head and kept walking. I walked and walked and walked until my frustration finally settled down. I don't know how long I walked, but I wanted to go say goodnight to Alicia, so I headed back to the hospital.

This time it was obvious that both Alicia and her mom were crying. As soon as I walked in Janice excused herself. I sat on the bed and hugged Alicia. "You left me," she cried.

"Left you? Oh no, I just needed to walk around. I didn't want you to see me upset," I explained without saying I really didn't want to cry in front of her.

"I don't blame you if you want to leave me, Ray."

"Well I do have to work in the morning and some nurse in the hall told me visiting hours are almost over."

"That's not what I meant. You didn't know what a handful I am. I would understand if you aren't up to this."

"What, you mean break up with you?"

Alicia nodded biting her lip and looking at me with big scared eyes.

"That thought never even crossed my mind," I answered honestly.

Alicia put her arms around me and held me really tight. "Please don't leave me," she cried into my shoulder.

I stroked her hair and folded my arms around her. "I'm not going anywhere, Alicia." I knew I was in deep. Very deep.

11 – POPCORN AND PEONIES

I had another night of restlessness, but this time I was plagued by nightmares. I dreamt I was drowning and woke up gasping for air. I managed to fall back to sleep, but then I dreamt my tooth was loose, and when I started wiggling it the tooth fell right out into my hand, only to then have all my teeth start falling out. I was relieved to wake up and feel my teeth still intact, but it was four in the morning and I couldn't get back to sleep. I read some, and then decided to go for a run before work because I was so antsy and there isn't much you can do at five a.m.

I put on my new running shoes I got from Thomas, along with my soccer shorts and a t-shirt. It was already warm outside even though the sun was just coming up. The air was heavy with humidity and there weren't as many people around as usual, but a lot of people were out who seemed to be on their way to work. I decided to run to the park. I don't really run like a jogger: I am used to playing soccer, so I started out too fast and had to slow down and find a pace I could sustain. My mind was busy thinking about Alicia and what a shock she had given me, but I really fretted about how much worse it could have been. I worried about the future and what was going to happen and felt really helpless and angry about it.

After showering and eating, I sent a text to her mom's phone. "How's she doing today?"

Janice texted back, "She is recovering well and they might release her tomorrow."

I texted, "Can you tell her I will visit after work?"

I waited a few seconds before seeing the text, "Hey, it's me. Yes, please come soon! I miss you! But sorry, no salsa tonight."

I forgot we had a date and couldn't believe how much things had changed since that good memory of dancing in her living room. I texted back, "Plenty of time for that. Just get better, Dream-Girl."

Work was easy. Don basically just walked the job with me and went over the plans and told me about the two new guys I would be in charge of on Monday. One was a young low-skilled general laborer, the other an experienced guy who Don said would be making a good wage – and that I should keep an eye on him to make sure he was earning it. "What about Lenny?" I asked.

"He's gonna have four guys under him."

"Whoa." That meant I wouldn't be working directly with Lenny for a while, but he would be close by if anything came up.

Don continued to go over specific plans for the week and

I asked some questions and took notes using the new clipboard he had given me. When Don showed me the architect's rendering of what the loft would look like when finished, I got really excited about it. When he told me we were done at noon, I was even more excited, since I was anxious to get to the hospital.

But I wanted to run a few errands first, like get a new backpack and return the one Louisa had lent me. I also planned to go by the flower shop. I knew they sold flowers at the hospital, but I'd rather give Tracy my business.

"Hey," she greeted me when I entered her store. "Let me guess: things have progressed to red-rose level?"

"Uh, well... maybe, but that doesn't seem appropriate right now. I'm not sure what I want today."

"Hmmm. I'm not sure how to interpret that." Tracy's voice changed from teasing to concern. She rose from her stool and asked, "What catches your eye?"

"Besides that tattoo on your side?" I teased her. Tracy was wearing a shirt that was shredded on both sides and I could see a tattoo on her torso. She pulled up her shirt to reveal a path of flowers going down her side, some of it obviously hidden under her shorts.

"This was my first," she offered.

"So you didn't just walk into a tattoo shop a little buzzed and pick a cute little butterfly off the wall. You went 'all-in' from the start."

"Yeah, that's my style," Tracy laughed.

"Hey, I don't think I ever told you how much I liked *The Buffalo Hunter*."

"You read that book?" She sounded surprised.

"Yeah, it was really good, really incredibly intense."

"I know, right?" Tracy pushed her glasses up her nose, a super-cute and nerdy gesture, and said, "I'm trying to write a book, you know."

"Yeah, you said that. How's that going?"

"I think it's good, but I could really use some feedback."

"I'll check it out. I'm not an expert, but I read a lot and I know what I like."

"Really, you will?" Her face got excited. "Can I email it to you?"

"I don't have a computer," I admitted.

"Well, I'll just print out the first chapter for you now. And if you want more you'll have to come see me. Oh, and to buy flowers for your girlfriend, of course," she added. Tracy went back behind the counter and started printing while I looked around. I thought about "What catches your eye?" and I kept going back to these pink and white flowers that were kind of big and round, like balls.

Tracy came back with a stack of papers and seeing what I was looking at said, "Peonies. They are beautiful. What is it that attracted you to them?"

"Well, they look really pretty, extremely feminine, and incredibly fragile."

"Touch one, Ray." I did and was surprised. The flowers looked like tissue paper, like they would crumble if I touched them. The petals themselves were very soft and delicate, but the flowers felt really hearty, like a dense ball, much stronger than I imagined.

"I love those flowers," Tracy said.

"Me too," and I handed her a twenty and let her do her magic with flowers and green leafy stuff and bows. I thanked my friend as I folded her other masterpiece in half and put it in my backpack. "Thanks for trusting me to read your book."

"Thanks for being interested," she smiled, and waved as I headed out the door.

I was happy Janice wasn't in the room when I walked in, but Alicia appeared to be sleeping. I sat down in the chair next to her and her eyes gently opened, "Hey," she said very slowly.

"Were you dreaming about me?" I asked, leaning over to kiss her.

I heard a voice from behind me say, "Watch out for her heart rate, young man!" and turned to see a woman who was smiling and obviously teasing me. She gestured to a machine and said, "She usually hovers around 70-80 beats per minute. If that goes over a hundred, I'm going to have to ask you to leave."

I laughed and apologized while Alicia and the woman I assumed was a nurse exchanged glances. "You must be Ray. I don't shake hands, trying to avoid spreading infection," she explained as she bobbed in a sort of curtsey. It made me happy to think Alicia had told the nurse about me, but I couldn't imagine why she had.

The woman pulled up a chair, which I still didn't understand, then explained, "My name is Margaret and I'm Alicia's therapist, at least while she is here and I hope after she leaves the hospital too."

"Well, she is covered by my insurance," Alicia teased. I could see she must like the woman and I was very relieved that a professional was talking to her about her situation.

"I have a talk scheduled with Alicia right now, which explains why Janice isn't hovering about. But I'd like you to stay for a few minutes."

"Okay, cool. Then I'll go get something to eat." I said, rubbing my abdomen. I was starving.

"Ray, thank you for the beautiful flowers," Alicia said in a softer voice that made me wish I had her alone.

"You're welcome, beautiful," I answered softly and picked up her hand and kissed it. "But who are all these others from?" I asked, trying not to sound jealous.

"The big one is from my work, the tulips from our family friends, the Winstons. You'll meet them, I'm sure."

"Alicia, I was hoping you could tell Ray how you are feeling about your heart attack."

Alicia immediately turned red and her eyes filled with tears as she looked down, "Aside from humiliated? Everyone at work is going to know there is something wrong with me. My coworkers will look at me differently, and... well, to be honest, I am relieved to take a leave of absence from school."

I didn't say anything and neither did Margaret.

"And, um, I know I have been downplaying this because my mom and dad are so upset with me, but I know how bad this is. I know..." Alicia hesitated and looked up at me, and then back at the sheet she was twisting in her hands, "I know if I was at home when this happened and not surrounded by people, well... It could have been way more serious. It is possible I could have even died."

I nodded but didn't speak. I couldn't speak with the lump in my throat anyway. It was exactly what I was thinking during my run that morning, about what might have happened if Alicia had been home alone instead of at work when this occurred.

"And, um, I don't expect anyone to believe me because I have said this all before, but I want to get better. I want to be healthy and not do this anymore. But I've said that before and my family won't believe me, but I do mean it, Ray." She had been speaking slowly, with hesitation, but the last few words spilled out in a rush.

"I believe you, Alicia. I just hope you can get better."

"Me too," she admitted. Then Margaret said, "Well, Ray, I hope to speak to you again, but I will talk to Alicia alone now, if you don't mind."

"Okay," I stood up and kissed Alicia gently on the lips and said, "I'll be back in an hour."

Alicia nodded, her eyes full of tears. I hated to see her so sad, but I was really glad she was getting therapy. Even if it didn't work in the past, I still had hope. I needed her to get well so bad.

After eating a sandwich in the cafeteria and killing some time reading, I went back up to the room to find Alicia alone, sitting up reading a book. "Whatcha reading?" I asked.

"Oh, one of my mom's cheesy romance novels," she laughed.

"Don't you like romance?" I asked.

"Well, yes, I admit I do. I would just be embarrassed to be seen reading this on the subway!" She held up the cover that showed a woman with her breasts pouring out of her dress being held by a man with long hair and a mask and we both laughed.

Alicia set the book on the nightstand and said, "Now that I am going to take a break from school, I'll have time to read again. Maybe you can recommend something?"

"Definitely. Or we can go see my friend William and he'll do this weird thing where he puts a hand on your forehead and figures out what type of book you need."

"Does he really do that?" she said with a giggle.

"Well, not exactly. But he does have a knack for picking books," I laughed. "We should go there when you are better."

"My life is going to look a lot different after this. I have not told my mom yet, but Margaret found me an outpatient program for eating disorders and I'm going to do that for three weeks."

"You're serious?" I felt my hopes rising.

"Yes, Ray. I really mean it, but I don't want to keep saying I am going to change. I need to show it. I know my parents aren't going to believe me and I won't have their support, and I don't blame them. But I really..." Alicia looked around the room before making eye contact again, "Well, I just hope I didn't blow it with you."

"You didn't blow it with me," I kissed her lips, and she wrapped her arms around me and pulled me in close, opening her mouth and kissing me back very hungrily, making it obvious she wanted more than light kissing. "Alicia! Keep your heart rate down, girl!" I was teasing, but looked at the machine just in case. It bounced around from ninety-five to one hundred, and as Alicia started kissing my neck I kept my eyes on the machine.

"She was joking," Alicia assured me. "I go over one-twenty every time I argue with my mom, don't worry. Don't deny me," she giggled.

I couldn't keep myself from worrying, but I couldn't help but respond to her sexy kisses and I wanted to feel what was under that hospital gown,... Ah-hah, no bra – just as I suspected! Alicia made a little moan in my ear and whispered, "I can't wait to get out of here and get you alone!"

I whispered back to her, "Oh yeah? What do you want to do to me?" I slipped a hand into the back of that open gown as I kissed her neck.

"Well, for starters, I've been thinking about the last time we were together. Remember we were in a hurry and I had to take a rain check on letting you go down on me?" She was breathing in my ear as my hand got low enough to confirm she was wearing panties, when all of a sudden I heard Janice say, "Hello! I'm baaaack!" in a sing-songy voice.

I sat up and turned around and Alicia straightened her gown and hair and said, "Hi, Mom."

"Hi, honey. Hi, Ray,"

I adjusted my pants as I sat down and said, "Hi, Janice, what's in the bag?" trying to distract her, hoping she wouldn't notice the bulge in my pants.

"Oh, just some things Alicia asked me to get from her apartment. Apparently she has a date tonight."

I looked at Alicia and she was grinning at me, "Well, since we can't go salsa dancing, I asked Mom to bring my laptop so we can watch a movie and eat hospital food together. Mom is going out with a friend tonight."

"Really? You have friends in the city?"

"Yes, I have a friend who moved here some time back and we keep in touch. She wants to take me to dinner, so you two will have to get along without me." Janice was smiling as she removed Alicia's laptop, two candles, and a bag of already popped popcorn, and a pack of red vines from her bag.

"Thanks, Mom!" Alicia was smiling and on her best behavior and her mom seemed a bit happier too, probably with the belief she would be taking her daughter home soon. Janice was dressed up, looking nice, and I was glad she was getting a break from the hospital, but even happier that I got to be alone with Alicia. The two hugged, and then Janice patted my knee and said she'd see Alicia in the morning.

Alicia scooted over on her bed and asked me to join her as she started up her laptop. We turned the lights out and turned on the candles. The ambiance of the room was completely altered, but then a nurse walked in and yelled, "What are you doing? You can't have an open flame in here!" She grabbed for the candle and Alicia told her, "They aren't real!"

The nurse picked up the candle and inspected it and still had a frown on her face as she noticed the candles were actually battery operated flickering lights. "They look pretty authentic, don't they?" I asked, hoping to lighten her mood.

"Yeah, well, you two little lovebirds nearly gave me a damn heart attack. What the hell is going on in here? Did I interrupt something?" She now had a half-grin on her face as she eyed us both.

"We were supposed to have a date tonight, so now we are having one here."

"Hmmm, I see. A romantic date right here in my hospital." She emphasized the word my. She put the candle back. "Lucky for you two I am a sucker for romance. But I have to turn on the lights while I fill out this chart."

"Thank you," we both said simultaneously, then grinned at each other as the nurse sighed and rolled her eyes in exaggeration.

We started up a movie and Alicia put her head on my shoulder as I had my hand on her thigh, but I stayed on top of the covers. We were interrupted by the nurse several times throughout the movie, as she kept coming in and making notes on a clipboard after looking at the machine on the side of the bed. She kept teasing us and calling us lovebirds. If we were lovebirds, then a single hospital bed was our nest.

Tension arrived with the dinner tray. The nurse said she was able to swing an extra meal for me, which was really nice of her. I had planned to go get something from the cafeteria, but I would never turn down a free meal. It was chicken and vegetables and rice and it looked pretty healthy to me, but Alicia had a furrowed brow and just stared at her plate. I almost offered to get her a salad from the cafeteria, but I didn't think that was the right thing to do. Alicia took a deep breath and said, "I am going to eat this and digest it and be okay."

"Of course you are," I said casually.

"That's my new mantra; that is what Margaret wants me to say."

"Margaret's a fucking genius," I said, laughing because I didn't really think it was a very profound mantra, but knew Alicia probably needed it.

Alicia ate about eighty percent of the food on her tray but said she couldn't finish the rest, and the nurse told her she had done really well. She didn't eat the popcorn, but she had two red vines and I noticed I had become hyper-sensitive to her discomfort around food and acutely aware of everything she ate. I hoped this wouldn't be permanent, because life is challenging enough without letting someone else's eating affect me so much.

We ended up watching two movies and then the nurse came and kicked me out saying visiting hours were over, and I kissed my Dream-Girl goodnight.

"See you tomorrow?" she asked.

"Of course. Here or at home?"

"I'll text you from my mom's phone." I kissed her again until the nurse swatted me on my backside and told me to get out.

I woke up early, relieved that I didn't have nightmares or insomnia. But waking up at five on a Sunday morning is harsh and completely unnecessary. I decided to work out and run again, especially since I hadn't been playing soccer lately. I did my sit ups and push ups and even some sets of pull ups on the bar I had attached in the bathroom doorway. Then I laced up my shoes and headed out the door.

I paced myself a lot better this time, but my mind was still running crazy. I was relieved that Alicia was planning to get help for her eating disorder, but I was really worried it wouldn't work. I knew she had tried this type of help before and wasn't convinced it would be different. Ten years was what Janice said. That hit me hard. I didn't want to get my hopes up, but hope was all I had. Without hope I had nothing. Actually, I had worse than nothing. I had fallen in love with Alicia and she was very sick. The realization felt like a punch in the gut, and it made me stop running to catch my breath.

I was almost back to my apartment and decided to walk the rest of the way. As I passed by the Catholic church, on an impulse I stepped inside. Mass had not started yet and I was feeling desperate enough to talk to God about all this. I knelt in front of a statue of Jesus and bowed my head, not really sure what to say, when I felt the presence of someone next to me. I looked to my side and saw the cute little old lady fashionista who had escorted me to the rummage sale a while back. While I was on my knees and she was standing, I was almost her height. "May I join you?" she whispered. I scooted over and held my hand out to help her kneel. "Who are you praying for today?"

"Alicia."

Still holding my hand, she closed her eyes and started praying out loud, "Lord, I don't know what Alicia needs, but you do, so Ray and I are asking that you pour your love on her and give her just what you think she needs. And bless Ray too, because he cares about her and he is hurting. Amen."

She squeezed my hand and didn't let it go. I felt really emotional, so I didn't speak for a few seconds until I felt I could. "Thanks. That wasn't a very Catholic prayer."

"I like to free-style it sometimes," she winked at me. I really liked this lady.

I stood and offered my hand to help her up. "Are you staying for Mass?" she asked.

"Uh, no, not dressed like this." I gestured to the clothes I had been running in.

"Oh Ray, nobody gives a damn," she said, reminding me of her penchant for cussing in church. "Besides, I've seen you look much worse." I looked at her expectantly and she went on, "You used to come in when the weather was bad and sit in the back with your hat pulled low."

I was stunned. She noticed me in my homeless state? She actually recognized and remembered me? "I thought I was invisible." I said it out loud.

"Nope. God sees everything, and I see plenty."

I laughed, and that is how I got persuaded to stay for Mass that day.

It was after eleven when I finally heard from Janice, not Alicia. She said Alicia was having another EKG and if all went well she would be released in a few hours. She suggested I wait and just meet them at Alicia's apartment. No more hospital! I felt my shoulders relax and realized how much I hated hospitals and why.

I went over late in the afternoon. Alicia's tiny apartment felt pretty cramped with the three of us there and her mom's big suitcase on the floor. Janice might have felt the same way because within five minutes of my being there, she said she was going to the drugstore to get Alicia's medication and pick up some groceries so we could eat at home.

There was no privacy to be found, so Janice said right in front of Alicia, "Keep an eye on her. Don't let her go into the bathroom alone. I mean it, Ray. And if anything happens, call 911 then call me on my cell." Alicia rolled her eyes as I agreed to Janice's request. When she walked out the door, Alicia went over to the window, apparently to make sure her mom was gone. Satisfied when she saw her on the sidewalk, Alicia turned to me and grinned and started unbuttoning her shirt.

"Hey, baby," I said slowly, "Are you sure?"

"Way beyond sure," Alicia answered, sauntering towards where I was sitting on the stool, unbuttoning as she came closer.

She stopped halfway across the room and pulled her shirt off and tossed it aside. Then she turned back and undid her jeans and lowered them slowly, swaying her hips from side to side as she worked them down. My Dream- Girl was putting on a show for me, a sexy, seductive show of getting naked, letting me take her in now as she turned around slowly revealing her entire beautiful form, only covered in matching bra and panties. Alicia brought a hand to her face, doing the simultaneously bold and shy thing that I loved about her, and then she reached both hands behind her back to unhook her bra and free those beautiful breasts I had not seen for a few days. She swung the bra around in a circle over her head playfully, and tossed it at me with a giggle.

Then she shimmied out of her panties, very slowly, revealing almost everything I wanted to see. It was so erotic and provocative, stripping for me, putting on a show, demonstrating how incredibly sexy she is without even touching me. When she turned her back again and stretched, reaching her hands in the air, she next bent over to touch her toes, and gave me a flash of pink that my eyes zeroed in on. She paused for a few seconds, gently swaying her butt in the air.

I was fully dressed and straining against my jeans, drinking her in with my eyes, and wanting to touch her, but not wanting to interrupt this beautiful display of sexiness. I expected her to come to me and be engulfed in my arms, but she stepped over to the futon and sat on the edge and parted her knees, revealing everything I wanted to see. I was torn between pouncing on her, and letting her continue her sexy show. Alicia closed her legs and smiled shyly, then opened them further.

She ran a hand seductively over her own breast and continued to open and close her legs. "Well, what are you waiting for?" She was grinning and had a fingertip at her mouth. I stood and peeled my clothes off, not trying to be sexy, just trying to get naked before taking the four steps that separated me from her parted legs.

I dove in, head first. I didn't even kiss her. Well, I did, but it went straight to the sweet spot between her legs, which was unlike me and caused Alicia to yell an uncustomary, "Fuck!" which startled me for half a second and made me question my direct approach, but the hand she immediately planted on the back of my head told me I had landed correctly. She was unusually expressive, not loud, just very verbal – and I loved it. Alicia moaned, and bucked and pulled my head in and her rants ranged from incomprehensible mumblings, interspersed with very direct approval, to groans of ecstasy. I kissed, and licked, and sucked, and even bit gently as she moaned and encouraged me with, "Yes! Yes! Yes!" And then: "Give me your finger, please!"

"I gave her two, which caused her thighs to clamp down on the sides of my head and her hips to lift off the futon, and she muffled a scream with her hand, then covered my face with waves of wetness as her thighs pressed tightly against my ears. I heard my girl moaning my name over and over, and my cock leapt in response. When she finally quit moving and lay there panting, I felt a joy I had never felt before. I wish I could say I was simply happy that she was happy, too, but making my girl cum like that was the best feeling ever. It made me feel powerful, like I could finally do something for her, something no one else could do. I had my head resting on her thigh and mindlessly lifted my hand to her heart to feel it beating.

"Don't worry, Ray, I'm not going to have another heart attack," she laughed, "but you are in big trouble now."

I looked at her to see why I was in trouble and Alicia smiled at me and said, "I'm going to want that all the time."

I laughed and got up on my knees to hug her not even caring if I got to enter her, but she reached over for a condom and let me put it on this time. "We'd better not take too long! Just in case my mom..."

I wasted no time and entered her sweetness as I was still kneeling between her legs and continued kissing her. Alicia wrapped her legs around me and kissed me back passionately, with an open mouth, licking my lips, sucking my tongue, even gently biting me as I worked my way in and out of her again and again and again. My hands reached under her butt and lifted her and I ground her into me as I continued my thrust. She was squeezing me with everything, her arms, her legs, her sex, and I exploded into her with a velocity and force that consumed me – and I didn't try to stay quiet about it either. I was overcome with euphoria as she clenched me and responded in kind, and I was surprised she was coming again, but then again she is absolutely the hottest woman ever, and so incredibly sexy. When she finally stopped bucking and laid her back down, I stayed inside but hovered over her just looking at her beautifully flushed face.

"I can't believe how good you make me feel," I told her.

"We are amazing together," she answered, then bit her lip like she wanted to say more. I brushed her hair off her sticky forehead and felt the pulse at her neck, and she laughed but brushed my hand away, "Stop worrying, Ray! I asked the doctor if I could have sex!"

"Really? And you got the okay?"

"She told me not to be on top," Alicia laughed. "At least not for a week. Seven days from now I'm going to the rodeo!"

"And I'll be your bucking bronco," I laughed.

"Yee-haw," she whispered, right before I kissed her pretty lips.

Just then the damn intercom rang. Dammit, I knew I shouldn't resent Janice. She was just there to help, but we had to jump up and get dressed and I went to the bathroom and there was no door knob on the door. That seemed strange. I was about to ask what happened, but when I came out Alicia and her mom were standing in the main room and they seemed to be in a heated argument.

Janice was saying in a strained voice, "Well, imagine my embarrassment when I made the pharmacist call the doctor! I thought he had made a mistake."

"It isn't that big a deal, Mom."

"You say that about everything, Alicia. I don't know why you can't just follow doctor's orders!"

"It wasn't 'doctor's orders,' Mom! She asked if I wanted anti-depressants and I said no. I'm not depressed! The only thing I am supposed to take is that Digoxin and the potassium tablets, and she said no problem with the birth control."

Did I just hear 'birth control'? We hadn't discussed it, but I got pretty excited at the idea of riding Alicia bareback.

"But you don't need them!" Janice was raising her voice, "Why do you need birth control when you are moving back to California!"

"What!" I exclaimed, in a voice so loud it surprised me. "What? You are what? Oh no!" I demanded, "Alicia, is this true?" I looked at Alicia who appeared horrified and was slowly but emphatically shaking her head no.

"You didn't tell him?" Janice yelled at Alicia. Then she turned to me and calmly stated, "I'm sorry you have to hear it from me, Ray, but yes, Alicia is moving home. We can't trust her out here alone."

"She's not alone!" My voice rose in both pitch and volume. "Alicia! You can't go!" She stood there staring at me gently shaking her head with her eyes full of tears and I wanted to shake her. I felt sick and angry at the same time, as if I had been kicked in the gut. I really wanted to punch someone, but there was no one in the room I wanted to lash out at, so I glanced at the brick wall, fuming, trying to calm down. I had almost lost Alicia, and now to find out I was going to lose her anyway? I was so overcome with feelings of anger and helplessness that I was literally shaking and didn't know what to do with myself. I started pacing in the tiny space with my fists clenched.

Alicia was crying now, but I didn't feel sorry for her. I was so mad at all the pain she was causing me. I couldn't believe that we had just made love like that and the whole time she was planning to leave and didn't even mention it. "What was your plan? When were you going to tell me?" I snapped at her, my voice coming out a lot louder than I intended.

"Mom," Alicia said quietly, "I'm going to talk to Ray for a minute, outside. I'll be back in a few minutes." I walked out the door, not even wanting to have this conversation, not wanting to hear Alicia break up with me and tell me how it was not me and all that crap. God, I was pissed. I rushed down the stairs and felt like just walking, but Alicia followed me out and grabbed my arm as I headed down the stoop and pulled me back. "Ray!" she whispered urgently, "I'm not leaving! I'm not going back to California, I promise."

She hugged me really tight and I pulled back enough to put my forehead on hers and say, "You can't go back, Alicia, you can't. I'm completely and hopelessly in love with you."

A startled look crossed her face. This wasn't how I had

planned to tell her how I felt about her, but I couldn't keep it in. Then the corners of her mouth turned up and even though she was crying, she said, "I know, Ray. I'm completely and hopelessly in love with you too. There is no way I would leave you." I hugged her tighter, and then loosened my grip to wipe her tears with my thumbs and then kissed her cheekbones over and over. I held her for several minutes until I could speak, "That scared the hell out of me. I'm sorry I yelled at your mom."

"I'm not," Alicia laughed, still sniffling tears. "My parents are going to cut off my financial support. They think I can't stay without their money, but I'm going to work it out, Ray. I promise you, I'm not leaving New York. I'm not leaving you.'"

I sighed deeply. I knew we had some big obstacles in front of us, but now I knew without a doubt how much Alicia meant to me, and I knew she loved me too. I didn't feel hopeless anymore and I didn't want to punch anything. I felt overwhelming happiness, but still had a knot in my gut, probably from this rollercoaster I was on. "I'd better go say sorry to your mom."

Alicia laughed and said, "Okay, but it's my dad I'm really worried about. He's coming in two days and he thinks he is packing me up and taking me home."

"No more, Alicia, no more. Now I'm the one who's going to have a heart attack," I half-joked with my hand on my chest.

"I'm so sorry for all this, Ray." She whispered, looking so beautiful and remorseful.

"You can make it up to me later," I teased her, and then changed my tone to make it clear, "I really do love you."

"I love you too, Ray! I really, really do." And we kissed once more before going upstairs to make peace with her mom.

12 – DRESSING ON THE SIDE

Alicia's dad looked like a lumberjack in a golf shirt, and his personality took up even more space than his frame. I met him along with Alicia and her mom at a restaurant the one night there was an overlap in her parents' visits. "Steve Klaer, Alicia's dad," he said, shaking my hand firmly and smacking me on the back simultaneously. Damn, he was intimidating. He had a barrel chest, a short beard, a loud voice, and a big smile. I could see that Alicia got her mouth and nose from him and her coloring from her mom.

Steve had a gregarious personality and teased his wife and daughter when not talking to me. I asked about his business. "Garage doors," he said. "I didn't plan on it. Want to guess what my major was in college?"

He didn't give me a chance to answer and I wasn't sure if splitting wood was a major. "History! Hell, I didn't know what I wanted to do with my life, but I got a job doing sales out of college and then Janice and I bought our first house, a real dog, a fixer-upper. But I couldn't find a garage door I liked so I created my own. I've always had a knack for working with my hands. Next thing you know the neighbors start asking me to build them one, so I start working out of that garage and one thing leads to another until twenty-five years later I am the biggest fabricator of custom garage doors in California, Nevada, and Arizona."

"Wow. I didn't even realize there was a need for custom garage doors."

"Well, we've got some impressive real estate out there, but then the recession hit and thank God I had the foresight to diversify and didn't stick to just residential doors. We started installing aluminum roll up doors and you know how we made it through the recession?"

Again he didn't wait for me to answer.

"Storage units. Hell, people in California started losing their homes or downsizing, but they didn't want to give up their stuff. Storage units started popping up like crazy in the desert communities. We'd get these jobs for a couple hundred doors at a time. So what about you? Alicia told me you're in construction."

"Yes," I answered, "We are working on a loft conversion right now. I love it."

"Ray is a supervisor already!" Alicia interrupted, but I didn't mind. "And he is only twenty-two! And he's amazing at soccer, and a really good dancer, and he reads all the time, and – "

"Dancer!" Steve asked in mockery, but he was smiling. "Ballet?"

"Salsa, smart ass." It was Janice who intervened.

"Well, you sure have won over the Klaer women, young

Ray-salsa-dancer-extraordinaire!" He was laughing and teasing me, but I didn't care. I was totally taken aback by Alicia bragging about me like that. She made me sound like such a good catch, I couldn't believe it. I shuddered to consider what Steve would think if he knew his daughter had hugged a guy out of near homelessness.

I looked over at Alicia who smiled back at me. She looked really pretty with her hair up and these drooping-down dangly earrings. I admired her long neck for a few seconds, and then went back to her eyes. "What, Ray?" she smiled shyly.

I told her what I was thinking. "You look especially pretty tonight." She smiled at me and brought her hand to her face. I wasn't even considering her parents at that moment, but they were watching us and not saying anything until Steve said, "I guess it's going to be pretty hard for you two to say good-bye." There was a pause in conversation, but Alicia and I maintained eye contact.

"Maybe Ray can come out for a visit when he can get some time off," Janice suggested. Alicia was still looking at me and even though we weren't speaking, I felt like I was reading her mind and she was telling me not to worry. Then I felt her bare foot caressing my shin. Steve and Janice started talking about the business and their other daughters and the logistics of moving everything back while Alicia and I remained quiet. I noticed some stress as they talked about the grandmother staying with the teens and about how they were both missing work. I really was getting a sense of what a big deal this was to their whole family and I felt anxious about Alicia telling her dad she wasn't going home. She already told me she was going to wait until her mom left to have that scary conversation.

The waitress brought our food and I saw Alicia tense up. She stared at her plate and whispered, "I asked for my dressing on the side." Steve got an irritated look on his face and Janice started looking around for the waitress and Alicia said, "No, Mom, it's okay. I'm going to eat this food and digest it and be okay." I smiled

197

hearing her mantra, but her parents didn't seem to notice.

After eating I had my hand resting on Alicia's and she was stroking my leg with her bare foot again. Steve glanced at my hand and said, "We are going to be really crowded in that little apartment tonight. Not to mention the fact that I have missed my lovely wife." He put his hand on Janice's shoulder and she smiled at him. "Alicia, why don't you stay at Ray's tonight? We will come and get you early in the morning, on the way to taking your mom to the airport."

Alicia looked at me beaming and I'm sure I was smiling just as big. Alicia excused herself to go to the restroom and Janice immediately jumped up to follow her, leaving just me and Steve at the table. "Don't let her go in the bathroom alone," he warned me. "I'm serious."

"Okay," I agreed. I wanted to say more. I wanted to tell him that I loved her and would take good care of her, but I couldn't. He still believed she was going back to California with him. We would need to have that conversation later.

We said goodbye to her parents and Alicia and I got into our own taxi. Alicia attacked me as soon as we were alone in the cab. "I've wanted to kiss you all night," she whispered in my ear, with her hand roaming the front of my pants. "Do you have condoms at home?"

"No, but there is a little market a few doors down from me."

"Good. I want to get a toothbrush and leave it at your place." She kissed my neck but I was not very responsive. I was busy worrying about what she might think of my apartment, but at least it was clean. When we got home, I opened the door and Alicia stepped inside and said, "Whoa, did your roommate take everything with him?" My place was spotless, but sparse with just a futon, coffee table, and a few books on a shelf.

"Yeah, he took everything," I laughed, not really explaining that everything was taken long before he moved out, or that there were two of them.

"Next time there is a rummage sale, we should go get some stuff for your walls."

"Good idea," I agreed. Alicia went to the bathroom and I followed her. "What are you doing?"

"I promised your dad."

"No, Ray. We are not going to do that. I am not going to let that start with us. You have to trust me."

"But I promised your dad."

"No, you have a relationship with me, not my dad. We are not going to start that pattern," she said sternly. "Do you really think I can be watched all the time? Ray, I am going to get better because I want to. Monitoring what I eat or following me into the bathroom doesn't work. My parents should know that by now, but they don't."

"They're just worried about you, babe. I am too."

"I know, I'm sorry," her voice softened. "But Ray, you cannot go in the bathroom with me. I promise to be out in thirty seconds."

And she was. Completely nude. "Wow," I took her in with my eyes, completely blown away that Alicia was standing in my apartment in all her naked glory.

"Let's get you naked too," she said, and dropped to her knees in front of me and started undoing my belt buckle.

I pulled my shirt off while Alicia worked on my pants. This evening was going so much better than expected, I couldn't believe it. Thirty minutes ago we were having dinner with her parents. Now Alicia was nude in my apartment kneeling in front of me. I looked down at my Dream-Girl and admired her beautiful backside as she freed me from my pants.

"Whoa," I exclaimed as she took me in her mouth, my pants still slumped around my ankles. I closed my eyes and lost myself in the feeling of her warm wet mouth caressing me over and over. She had a vise grip on me and her other hand on my butt. I stroked her silky hair and opened my eyes, feeling overwhelmed with lust and love, two feelings I didn't know could coexist. She was taking me more deeply into her mouth and started massaging my balls at the same time, then she backed her head up and began doing long licks, long strokes while looking up at me.

"My knees are sore," she giggled, so I stepped out of my pants and put my hands under her arms and lifted her up and kissed her fervently. Alicia lifted a leg around me so I used both hands to lift her butt so that she was completely off the ground, both legs around me.

"Wow, you're so strong."

"And you're so hot," I said as I lifted her up a little higher, then lowered her down onto me. I was surprised I could do that standing up and didn't know how long I could maintain it, but it felt amazing to have her engulf me with all her hot and tight goodness without a condom. Without a condom... Uh-oh. "How long until the pill works?" I asked.

"A few weeks," she answered, lowering her leg so that I squatted and sat her down. She retrieved a condom from her purse and put one on me and I was planning to lift her again, but she stepped over to the futon and put both hands on the back and bent over. God, I loved having her in my apartment.

I held her hips in my hands and Alicia gasped as I entered her from behind, "Oh my god, Ray, you feel so amazing!"

"So do you," I answered, kissing the back of her neck and reaching around to squeeze her breast. She backed her butt into me with every thrust and reached her own hand down between her legs to apply more pressure, leaving my hands free to roam her beautiful body as we moved in unison. She was squirming her butt around like crazy and I grabbed her hips again to slow her down. I couldn't last with her moving like that but she moaned and begged so I let her loose again and she started wiggling again, reminding me who was the boss. I would do anything for her. Anything.

She was backing into me in a side-to-side motion that felt really incredible. Alicia started clenching and squeezing me in a way that was blowing my mind and when she cried out in pleasure, I let myself go and just enjoyed her clenching that was milking every drop out of me. Alicia's legs started twitching in a way I had never seen before and it almost scared me for a second, but then she collapsed on the couch and was laughing with giddiness and exclaiming, "Oh my god, how can that be? It just keeps getting better!"

"I know, right? Maybe because we are getting more comfortable with each other."

"Then imagine what it will be like a year from now," she said.

"You'll be sick of me by then," I assured her and Alicia rolled over and looked at me.

"You must be kidding," she said. "You're the best thing that ever happened to me, Ray. I am the one with all the issues. I hope you don't get sick of me. But you have given me great motivation to get better."

I stroked her cheek and moved her hair out of her face. I felt dishonest allowing her to think I am some great guy with a good job and no issues and that she was the one with all the problems. I didn't plan on it, but I told her. I told her everything –

about my year of near homelessness and about Thomas and Jeff and how I was depressed. I told her about how I didn't comb my hair and it got all matted and how I sometimes went days without uttering a single word to another human being. I told her about how I slept at the park or at libraries, and how I ate food that people left on their trays and how sometimes I was so hungry I would watch someone throw food in the trash then retrieve it. I told her about how lonely I was and how I felt invisible.

"Well, that explains it," Alicia answered matter-of-factly.

"Explains what?"

"Why you seem so much older than twenty-two. You've seen a lot and been through a lot and that is probably why you are the way you are. So kind. Not judgmental."

I looked down at her dumbfounded. "You mean to tell me that you see my past as an asset? You could love a guy who ate out of trashcans?"

"Pfff," Alicia made a noise and waved her hand. "Yeah I can. Can you love a girl who puked in jars?"

I looked at her with question marks in my eyes and she went on, "When I was sixteen, my parents put a padlock on the bathroom door so that I couldn't go in there and throw up. My sisters and I would have to go into their bathroom at night where they could hear us. But I got around that. I would save empty jars and keep them in my closet, then puke into them and put the lid back on. The thing was, I couldn't put them in the trash where my mom would see them, so they started stacking up in the back of my closet. I must have had thirty jars full of puke stacked up against the wall and one day my mom found them. Can you imagine how horrifying that was for her? That is when they sent me to the residential program."

"Oh my god, that is so sick," I said. I couldn't help it, it just came out and I couldn't pretend not to be disturbed. Thankfully, Alicia started laughing.

"Oh yeah, it really was. But you should talk, Mr. Eats-Out-of-Trashcans! I'd say we are pretty even," and she was laughing and so was I. I kissed her and told her I loved her even though she was totally disgusting and she laughed and said it was mutual. I couldn't believe how great I felt. I didn't know keeping that secret from Alicia was such a burden and now I didn't have to worry about what she found out or if she would reject me. She must have felt the same relief. We were both lying there naked, more naked than we have ever been now that our secrets were out.

"I won't follow you into the bathroom or get on you about your eating, but I do want to know about the scratches on your hands."

"Sticking my hand down my throat, making myself gag."

I shuddered. I pictured something much daintier, like a finger gently going into her mouth, but now I had an insight into the violence that she inflicted on herself. I hugged her tighter.

"Don't worry, Ray. I told you because I don't want to keep doing it."

"I know, babe." I kissed her forehead, hoping she could close the gap between wanting to stop and actually stopping.

We were standing out on the sidewalk when Alicia's parents pulled up in a cab. I said goodbye to Janice and gave Alicia a quick kiss before heading off to work. Today I was teaching Joe, the new guy, how to remove the bathroom fixtures. He seemed like a hard worker, but he lacked skills. He needed a lot of practice and he was nervous with me watching him, so I stepped away to look at my phone.

Alicia and I had not made plans for that evening and I figured that she was going to do something with her dad, but I got a text saying she told him and her dad was really pissed, worse than she expected.

I asked if she wanted me to come over and she wrote back "Yes. He wants to talk to you."

A feeling of dread came over me, so I tried to just focus on work until it was time to go.

After showering, I walked over to Alicia's house, trying to be calm and not worry about what her dad might want to say to me. I stopped in at Tracy's flower shop, but not to buy flowers. She was busy making an arrangement and there was a customer in the shop, but she stopped to talk to me.

"Hey, no flowers today, but I just wanted to tell you how much I liked your writing. I was wondering if it would be okay if I let my friend William read it too. I'm interested to hear what he has to say. He's a librarian and really knows books more than anyone I know."

"Really? That would be great! I could use all the help I could get." Tracy turned to her computer and started the printer, "But I want to hear what you think about it!"

"It's really good. I made some notes on the margins and I want to give it back to you and take the next chapter, but I didn't bring it with me."

"Oh, that's okay. I am so excited about it! I just joined a writer's group that meets at the library twice a month! Tomorrow's my first day!"

"Agnes?"

"No, Mid-Manhattan."

"That's where William works. What time is it over? I'll just meet you there."

"Eight o'clock." Tracy answered and handed me a fresh stack of papers.

"Cool. I love that library. I'll see ya then."

Alicia's little apartment felt tiny with Steve Klaer in it. He took up a lot of space and paced around and made waving hand gestures in the air and I kept thinking he was going to accidently knock something over. He wasted no time telling me what was on his mind. "So Alicia's trying to convince me it is a good idea for her to stay in New York, but obviously she doesn't know what's good for her. I can see that you two have gotten pretty close and you're at least part of the reason she wants to stay here, but I just can't have that. How do you think if feels to be three thousand miles away while your little girl is killing herself?" He didn't wait for an answer to his rhetorical question. "So I've been thinking, Ray: you seem like a nice enough guy and Alicia's crazy about you, so why don't you come to California and work for me? I'll start you out in sales until you learn the business – that's the best way to learn it. And rents are high, but no higher than here and you'd have more space." He gestured to the room with his hands spread wide.

I looked over at Alicia and her eyes were big. I got the impression it was the first time she had heard her dad's master plan. Steve stared at me expectantly and I didn't know what to say. I was caught completely off guard. "You mind if I talk to Alicia alone for a minute?"

"Sure, go ahead."

"We'll step outside," Alicia spoke. "I need some air."

"Fine. Talk it over. Tell him about the weather and... and... tell him about surfing."

Alicia and I walked outside and when we got to the stoop we sat down on the step.

"Wow. I wasn't expecting that," I admitted.

"I wasn't either," Alicia replied. "That was an interesting chess move."

"Well," I said slowly, carefully choosing my words, "It is pretty obvious your dad loves you, Alicia. You're lucky to have a family that loves you so much."

"Yes," she answered thoughtfully. "Too much sometimes. I mean, I appreciate what he is trying to do, but I've been talking to my therapist Margaret about this. It's really time for me to grow up and quit taking from them anyway. I know this is going to be really hard on them, but I can't go back and live under their wings. That's one of the reasons I want to stay, so I can show them they don't have to worry about me, but it's going to take a long time to win that trust. I couldn't do it with them hovering over me, stealing door knobs, making me get on the scale and all that stuff. Besides... I love New York. I love you."

I put my arm around her and said, "I love you too, Alicia. And I can't see myself being any good at sales."

Alicia laughed, "Garage doors, Ray! Come on, get excited! And then there's surfing!"

"Yeah, well, I'll bet it is a nice place to visit, but I'm really starting to like my life here," I said, just realizing it for the first time myself. "Yeah, I got some good stuff going on, I don't want to start over. Plus, to be honest, I don't like the idea of being under your dad's wing either."

"But there's surfing!" Alicia teased me, smiling. "Surfing,

Ray."

I don't know why we thought that was so damn funny because I'd never even thought about surfing before, but it did sound ridiculous and we were both cracking up.

"Well, how are we going to work this out?"

"I am going to work it out, Ray. I mean, I want your emotional support, but I don't want you to try to fix this. I have already made some big changes and I'm going to be okay. I told my boss I'd like to work full time and he was really happy about it. After my leave of absence, of course. I am definitely going to do that outpatient program Margaret got me into."

"Will you be able to afford your apartment without your parents' help if you work full time?"

"Probably not. But I am open to moving and sharing an apartment. But not with you, Ray."

I laughed, "Well, I was going to offer."

"I thought you might, and I would love to live with you someday, but not for this reason. I don't want you for a roommate yet; it's too soon for that. I want to date you."

Relief washed over me. I'd been thinking the same thing, that we might need to move in together just to save money, but I hated that reason. "We haven't even had that many dates yet. I want to take you salsa dancing as soon as you are well."

"I see the doctor tomorrow for a follow up. I'll see what she says."

"No rush. We've got all the time in the world."

"Yes, we do," Alicia smiled at me and brought her face to mine for a kiss. I got really into kissing that pretty face and those soft lips, and then I remembered Steve was waiting for us upstairs.

"We'd better go face the music."

Alicia made a tense smile and we walked upstairs. His reaction to our news was like a natural disaster. A few of them, actually. First he exploded like a volcano. Then he ranted like a hurricane. Then he zeroed in on me like a lightning strike. "Do you think love can fix this, Ray? Well, guess what, Alicia has been loved her whole life! Love doesn't work on this!"

"What does?" I asked calmly and sincerely. It was a legitimate question, but it pissed him off.

"How the fuck do I know?" He yelled, throwing his hands in the air. Then he sat down on the stool and said very quietly in almost a whisper, "How the fuck do I know?"

I felt his frustration.

Alicia was sitting on the futon with her face in her hands and she looked up and said, "Daddy, you have to give me another chance. Please don't give up on me."

"Honey, you had a fucking heart attack," he said and his voice cracked. I got really nervous that he might cry and not want me there, but he sat up straight and his voice got stern again, "You've had so many chances, and this is what we get? A call from the hospital saying our little girl had a heart attack? Canceling our vacation plans? Rearranging everything to rescue you one more time, just to be told you'd rather stay in New York? Well, guess what, you've had your chance." And that is when it felt like an ice storm. There was nothing more to say.

He left the next morning and Alicia called me at work. I had told Don ahead of time I was expecting an important call, but as it turned out Don wasn't at the jobsite anyway.

"How are you doing?" I asked.

"Sad, but okay. I talked to Margaret and that helped. I understand they are going to be really upset for a long time. I need to show them I am changing, but that is going to take some time."

"Are you going to be okay? I mean like... this is the first time you've been alone, right?"

"Yes, I know what you're saying, Ray. I am not going to do anything stupid. I'm just cleaning up my apartment right now. It feels weird to have free time, to not be studying."

"Go to the library with me!"

"You and that library!" she laughed. "So this is your idea of dating?"

"We'll get dinner after," I assured her. "I need to see my friend Tracy and give her back her manuscript."

"Who's Tracy?"

"I'll tell you about her on the way. I've got to get back to work. Are you okay to meet me at the subway station? Did the doctor say walking is okay?"

"Yes, she encouraged it. She said no running yet, but pretty soon."

"Cool, I've been running too."

"You have? When?"

"A few mornings lately. Maybe we can run together when you get the okay?"

"Yes! I would love that!"

"Okay, bye, babe. I love you."

"I love you too!" she answered, right before I hung up and turned to see Joe the new guy drop a sink on his foot.

When I finally got through that hectic day and met Alicia at the subway station, I could see that she was melancholy about her dad heading back home to California on bad terms. As we sat on the train, I tried to cheer her up by describing the scene Joe the new guy, hopping around on his other foot, trying to avoid the dropped sink on the floor, and loudly calling on Jesus, Mary, and all the saints to help him. Luckily for me, it was a funny story because he didn't get seriously hurt. Just a bruise and a little soreness that would remind him to pay better attention in the future. I would hate to explain to Don how Joe smashed his foot while I was on the phone. Instead, Joe ended up apologizing profusely thinking he was the one in deep trouble. I told him not to worry about it, just try to be more careful next time. The poor guy seemed like a nervous wreck around me.

"Can you believe Don was so worried about the guys respecting me, and then Joe acts all intimidated around me? I almost feel sorry for him, but I have to watch out not to show it. I actually reprimanded him for trying to move the sink alone! But then I felt guilty about it and spent the rest of the workday trying to teach him the right way to do things – and that's frustrating. It's hard to watch him work when I could grab the tool out of his hand and do it myself in half the time. But that's probably the same thing Lenny would have say about me," I laughed.

"Is it something he can learn? Or do you think working with your hands is something that just comes naturally to some people?" She asked.

"Hmmm, I think people might be drawn to things they are good at, but of course you have to polish your skills. Some people can never draw or play sports or sing well no matter how much they wish to."

"Well, you're very good with your hands," Alicia put

special emphasis on the word "very" and then winked at me and leaned in closer to whisper, "And very good with your mouth."

I couldn't suppress a grin after that compliment and assured her that her skills were already top-notch, but she could practice on me as much as she wanted whenever she wanted.

We got off the subway and Alicia asked me about Tracy. "She owns the shop where I get you flowers and she's writing a book. She's in a writing group that meets at the library and I want to give her back the chapters she shared with me."

Alicia got a worried look on her face and I could sense that she might be having jealousy issues, but I didn't say anything to console her. I figured she could meet Tracy and see with her own eyes how it is.

We spotted William behind the desk engrossed in a stack of paper. "Hey," I greeted him. He came over and reaching over the counter said, "Two of my favorite New Yorkers! How are you this evening?" He took Alicia's hand in his.

"Great," I answered. "Alicia's got some free time in her schedule and needs a good novel."

"Or two," she added. "Are you busy?"

"I am climbing up this mountain of resumes searching for a new librarian, but nothing outranks friends and books in importance."

"Any good applicants?"

"Alas, too many: I am bedeviled with a superabundance of good options. They are mostly new graduates, and so I start by removing those with a grade point average of 4.0 from the stack."

"Why would you do that?" Alicia asked with concern.

"Well, my dear, if I have two candidates with similar

backgrounds in experience but one has a 3.0 GPA and the other has a 4.0, both would doubtless be more than capable of carrying out the requirements of the job. The difference is that the person with the 3.0 would likely have a disposition I prefer to work with."

"Oh," Alicia answered and appeared to drift into deep thought.

"Hey, we're gonna be here awhile. We're meeting a friend, but I wanted to see if you wouldn't mind having a look at this first chapter of a book she's writing," I pulled out of my backpack the copy Tracy had previously given me to share with William. "I think it's great, but I'd love to hear what you think and I'm sure she'd appreciate it too."

"I'd be honored," William replied, with a short, stiff bow.

We let William get back to work as I led Alicia over to the fiction section where I pulled her into the stacks and kissed her passionately while pressing her into the shelf. "Wow," she teased me, "libraries really do turn you on."

"You really turn me on," I said, kissing her once more before taking her hand and leading her to the H section. We had talked about books and because she said she wanted to start with something light and funny, I wanted to introduce her to the author Nick Hornby. Alicia agreed, but also said she wanted to find her own book so that she would be able to tell me about something I had not already read. I picked out a few titles for myself and we sat down to read and wait for Tracy. When not relying on William's recommendation, I usually read a page or two and tried to get a feel for a book and see if I like it before checking it out of the library. This probably goes back to my life on the street when I could only carry one book around with me. I started thinking about other ways the past year might have changed me and was deep in thought when William walked up waving Tracy's pages and said, "Ray, who is this author? Where did you find her?" He wore an exceptionally intense expression, and there was urgency in his tone of voice.

"Her name's Tracy. She owns a flower shop, and that's where I met her. Did you like it?"

"Like it? To say that I am favorably impressed is to put it mildly. I must know more about the beautiful soul who was able to conceive such an intriguing story, and then deliver it with such mastery and aplomb."

"Well, she's around here somewhere if you want to meet her. She joined a writers group that meets here."

"She's here now? Here in this library?" William looked around nervously. "She must be in the room with the 3FC Writers group. Ray, will you introduce me?"

"Sure," I said. "Alicia's going to meet her too. She said she'd be done at eight o'clock."

William looked at his watch, said, "I am going to read it again and gather my thoughts," and walked away briskly.

"Wow, that was kind of weird," Alicia whispered.

"I know, huh? It was like he has a crush on her without having even met her."

"Well whatever she wrote seemed to impact him, and he reads all the time."

"Yeah, I thought he'd like it, but that was more than I expected." Then I laughed lightly and mentioned to Alicia that they were not each other's type.

"How so?" Alicia asked.

"You'll see. Tracy looks like a girl who would date a guy in a rock band, not a librarian."

"Hmmm, as long as she's not into soccer-playing salsa

dancers, I'm sure we'll get along just fine."

I laughed, thinking maybe I was not too sure about Tracy's taste in men, and kissed my Dream Girl again. "I think we are setting a record for kissing in the library," I whispered in her ear. But then I remembered what a chick-magnet William is. The library has probably seen a lot of action.

Tracy was wearing red boots and a short black dress that showed part of her thigh tattoo. Her jet black hair and glasses made her look really intense and pretty at the same time. Alicia looked really soft-pretty next to her and the contrast of the two made each of them look even more attractive. When I introduced them, Alicia asked about the writing group.

"I'm really excited about it!" Tracy whispered, looking around to make sure none of the members were around. "Tonight I just heard them critique three people's writing and the feedback and insight was... well, a little intimidating, but I know it's going to be really beneficial!"

"So they didn't read your stuff yet?" I asked.

"No!" she said, "I am supposed to just observe the first time. Next time I will critique other people's work, and then I get to submit mine! Scary!" Tracy did a mini dance by stepping in place, "But just listening to them gave me some insight into some changes I need to make to improve my story."

"I wouldn't change a thing." It was William. He had joined our little group and Tracy looked at him in surprise.

"Oh hey, William," I said, turning to Tracy, "This is my friend William I told you about, the one I wanted to read your writing."

Tracy stuck out her hand and William shook it but didn't

hold on to it like he did with Alicia. "So what'd ya think?" Tracy asked casually.

William hesitated and I got ready for his fancy words to pour over Tracy like syrup, but instead all he said was, "Um, I thought it was... well, I loved it, but... I have so much to say I... I... I don't know what to say..."

"What?!?" I exclaimed. This was not what I expected at all. In fact, I was counting on William to put my thoughts into a coherent summary. Since when was he at a loss for words?

"Well, you did tell us you were blown away," Alicia injected, trying to reassure Tracy, who didn't know how to take William's reaction.

"Um... yes, well, yes... kind of knocked off my feet, and... well, I would really like to talk to you about it in more detail." Poor William actually seemed nervous.

"Well, hey, why don't you call me or email or something? When you are not busy at work?" Tracy pulled out one of her business cards and gave it to him. William held the card in his two hands and stared at it solemnly, reverently. "Did you draw the tiger lily?"

"I did. How'd you guess? Is it obvious?" Tracy laughed.

I looked over William's shoulder to check it out. I just assumed it was something she had bought. It was cool-looking. Dramatic and edgy – like her.

"I am... in the presence of a true artist. And I am at a loss..." he stammered.

"No worries, William. I don't mean to put you on the spot. Why don't you just email me when you get a chance? I'd love to hear your thoughts on my writing." And with that William said goodbye and swiftly disappeared.

"Wow," Alicia whispered. "That was so unlike him." After a short pause she added, "I think he's crushing on you, Tracy."

Tracy smiled and said, "Yeah, that was kind of weird. Well, I hope he does email me. He's actually pretty handsome – with a streak of nerd-appeal." And both girls laughed and nodded in agreement.

"Yeah, that was really weird," I stated, hoping the irritation in my voice wasn't obvious. I felt confused because William is such a womanizer and I didn't know if this was a game and I felt a little protective about Tracy. I took her writing out of my backpack and handed it to her, "Well, I don't know how to do a proper critique, but I made some notes on here. I point out parts I especially liked, or a few times I wanted to hear more. There was one thing that confused me."

"The sweater in the car? That was supposed to confuse you. That will make sense later."

"Oh, I should have trusted you," I laughed.

"Hey, Tracy, can I read it too?" Alicia asked.

"Of course! I'd love it! And either of you can pass it on to anyone you trust; you don't need to ask me. I'm not kidding: I am so excited that people actually want to read this!"

Tracy started to hand Alicia my copy, but Alicia said, "I don't want to see Ray's notes. I want my own impression to be fresh. Can you email it to me?" I watched as Tracy put Alicia's contact information in her phone and it occurred to me that Alicia didn't really have any girlfriends to hang out with. She had been busy working and studying all the time and now there was going to be a void in her life, one I couldn't fill all by myself. I wondered if I should ask Tracy to join us for dinner, but Alicia beat me to it, and Tracy said she needed to get home and wake up early to go to the flower market, so we said goodbye.

"I like her. She's cool," Alicia said over dinner. "And I was surprised that William was so smitten with her."

"Yeah, me too. I think he liked her before he even saw her."

"But she is really attractive."

"She is." I admitted.

"I keep thinking about what William said, you know, before he lost his voice," Alicia laughed then turned serious, "Remember, about not hiring a person with a 4.0? At first it seems ridiculous: after all, the better the grades, the better the person, right? But when I listen to William, he makes a lot of sense. I can see that I have been really caught up in my grades and... well... it made me... not a very nice person."

"I wouldn't say that, but I was starting to get stressed about your grades myself."

"I let a few points totally determine what kind of day I would have, or week. I was totally self-absorbed, and that made me hard to be around."

"No, you weren't," I tried to reassure her. It did sound like she was being too hard on herself.

"No, Ray, I know I was. You haven't known me long enough to really see how I could be. I have been like that for years and I always thought – I don't know – like I had to prove I was worthy. Now I am getting a glimpse into how irritating it was, always having to get A's and letting it rule my life."

I kept eating and realized Alicia had eaten all her food and I hadn't even thought about her eating. The realization made me smile as I continued to gaze at her. I kind of liked the idea of her not being stressed out with school, at least not for a while. Not only would she relax and enjoy life, we could date and enjoy each other's company. Also, I might not seem like such a slacker, lacking in motivation compared to her.

"Why are you smiling?" She asked.

"School will always be there for you. I am going to reveal my own selfishness now. I am really glad that you have to slow down and recover. It means I get to spend more time with you, getting to know you better, seeing how you really are when not trying to jump through hoops."

Alicia smiled at me and said, "That is funny because I was thinking something similar, about how I am going to have to get to know myself. I hope I like myself, Ray. I hope I like who I am when not creating my identity by always focusing on goals."

"Oh, you will," I laughed lightly, in quiet delight, not because it was funny. I understood the seriousness of what she was saying, but I felt confident in my answer and wanted to put her at ease. "I happen to know that you are extremely likeable. You are really sweet and smart and fun and everyone who meets you feels really comfortable around you."

"Really?' Alicia was smiling.

"Really. In fact, you are a very cool person, aside from being sexy and hot. If you had a clone, you would want to be friends with her. You'd probably love her. You might even turn gay, that is how lovable you are."

Alicia was laughing now and called me a pervert. "You'd like me to have a clone, wouldn't you?"

"You are enough for me, baby," I gave the right answer, then admitted the truth, "But oh my god, that would be so hot for one night." And with that I paid the bill and we walked to the subway station. When we got on the train, Alicia started whispering naughty ideas in my ear about what she and her clone could do to me. I don't know if I could really handle two clone dream-girls, but it sure was fun to think about.

13 – BREAD AND BUTTER

"Texas Toast? Alicia, calm down, tell me what's going on."

Alicia was explaining to me how she almost got kicked out of her recovery program that day. Apparently she refused to eat something called "Texas Toast" that I had never heard of, but she described it as frozen white bread dripping with saturated fat. It sounded like garlic bread to me, all buttery and tasty. She said she finally broke down and ate it, but cried and it was really hard for her and she almost walked out. I listened patiently thinking how I wished the hardest part of my day was eating garlic bread, but I didn't say that. Instead I surprised myself by saying I was proud of her for sticking it out. Texas Toast. Sheeze. I went up and down stairs hundreds of times carrying heavy loads in the heat and dealing with Joe, and Alicia had to eat "Texas Toast." It was making me hungry just hearing about it.

Alicia had started her outpatient program a week prior and on the first day I was waiting for her when she came off the subway. She was looking cute in her jeans and boots, but she also looked a little tired and stressed out. "Wow," she said, hugging me. "That was intense!"

"Tell me what it was like?" I probed.

"Well, first we had to eat breakfast together! Breakfast and lunch every day, Ray! And you have to eat whatever they serve unless you have some type of allergy that's already been documented in your file. Today wasn't so bad, but the girls told me it varies a lot. Once we ate, they immediately launched us into an activity, the idea being that we would be so busy doing something that we wouldn't obsess over what we just ate. Today they had us making these little gift baskets for people in a nursing facility. That part was kind of fun, actually. Then we had group therapy, then individual therapy, then lunch, then another activity -- journaling this time – and then a guest speaker came. The afternoons are always different, with some type of education or a guest speaker each day. Basically they keep us busy all day long, shuffling around and..." Alicia paused and took a breath, slowed down and met my eyes. "It wasn't that bad, Ray. It really wasn't bad at all. I am going to do this. And I met a girl who is pretty cool. A few of them aren't, but this girl Melanie and I got to talking and... It was good." She gave me a tired smile and I kissed her cheek.

During the walk home, Alicia told me she needed to talk to me about something and I got a little nervous. Something was bothering her enough that Margaret had instructed her to talk to me about it and she must have heard the trepidation in my voice because she said, "It's nothing bad, I promise. I just told her I would talk to you about it." I was feeling kind of shell-shocked by all the stuff going on and was relieved I wasn't about to have another bomb dropped on me, but when I got to her apartment, Alicia looked nervous.

"Sit down," she said, gesturing to the couch. I took a deep breath bracing myself.

"Margaret says I am doing really well with my therapy, but I have this one really big fear and she wants me to talk to you about it."

I kept quiet waiting for her to go on, but she hesitated. Finally, in a very small voice Alicia asked, "Are you going to stop loving me if I get fat?"

I hadn't thought about the possibility of Alicia getting fat, so I thought about it before answering. I couldn't imagine not loving her, but I couldn't really picture her fat either. I tried picturing her as a round little butterball with a couple of chins and I started grinning. But then I knew the truth and I wanted to be honest. "I am worried that if you got fat you would be miserable. Your personality would change. And I couldn't stop loving you, but if you couldn't walk around New York or go upstairs quickly, that would be tough."

"Not that fat, Ray! Oh my god, I could never get that fat and handicap myself. I meant what if I gained like... ten or fifteen pounds?"

I chuckled, "Oh well, that is a relief. Honestly, Alicia, I thought you meant FAT!"

"Well, that is fat!"

"Ten or fifteen pounds?" I switched over to my Sha-Nay-Nay voice, "Girl, that would just make you even more scrumptious and dee-licious! I would eat you up, slap a little butter on those buns, and take a bite!"

"I'm serious, Ray!" Alicia pouted.

"Alicia, you can't be serious. Ten pounds? Fat? Come on."

I was getting exasperated. Alicia didn't answer and I could see that she was serious. I realized I needed to educate her about something. "Mind if I use your computer? I trust you have virus protection?"

"Yeah, why?"

"I'm about to show you what sexy looks like to a guy." Alicia went and changed clothes while I searched for what I wanted to show her. It took a few minutes because I was out of practice, but soon enough I was navigating around a porn site looking for what I wanted her to see, still photos of real women. "There you go, what do you think of her?"

"Chubby?" Alicia asked.

"Nope, hot. What about this one."

"Boobs too small?"

"Nope, hot. Natural hot. And this one?"

"Oh, she is overweight for sure."

"Nope. She is hot for sure."

"Ray!" she laughed, "I'm starting to think you like them all!"

"Well, I am assuming they all have spectacular personalities," I grinned. "Now this one?"

"Oh, she has a fantastic body, I'd love to look like her."

"Yeah... but she looks hard. Kind of like a dude. She might work out several hours a day, but if it was natural, it would be okay. Now this one?"

"Oh Ray, you have to admit it: she's fat."

"She is HOT! Man, if Carlos saw this he would lick the computer screen."

"Seriously, Ray? Are you saying my butt could get that big and you would like it?"

"Baby, I'd use if for a pillow every night."

Alicia swatted me then said the next one looked good.

"She's too skinny. No hips. But her face is nice."

"You are a lot easier on the girls than other girls are."

"Exactly. Most guys are. You don't have to look like a Victoria's Secret model to be sexy, Alicia. Sexy comes in all shapes and sizes. You look amazing, but how you act has a lot to do with your sexiness. You are hot and beautiful and you have a lot of wiggle room before you could ever be considered even chubby."

"I am going to remind you of this conversation when you think my butt is big and don't want to have sex with me anymore!"

"I dare you to grow that butt!" I grinned at her, getting kind of turned on at the thought.

"Oh yeah, what would you do if I did?"

"Bury my face in it."

"Ray!" she squealed and swatted me again, then leaned in and kissed me, sweetly and slowly. "Well, can you make do with an average-sized ass for now?"

"Baby, there is nothing average about your ass," I said, and reached down to grab it and pull her on top of me. "I am going to show you what I think of this ass," I whispered in her ear, slipping my hand down inside her yoga pants and squeezing both cheeks firmly. Alicia moaned in my ear and whispered, "Ray, will you do what he is doing?" I looked up at the computer screen and saw that I must have hit a button because there was a video of a couple going at it and the guy was eating the girl from behind.

"Whoa," I laughed, "You are a naughty Dream Girl!"

But of course I was more than willing to fulfill her wish – which coincided with mine anyway – which was to bury my face deep into her with her cute butt sticking up in the air. It proved to be a very good angle that we both appreciated. Then Alicia informed me that I could skip the condoms since her pills had finally kicked in. I had slid into her without a condom a few times in the past, but had never stayed there very long and this time the sensation was all-consuming, overpowering. The combination of the porn, the oral sex, making her cum on my face, even the talk about her butt got me all worked up. But the feeling of skin on skin had me moaning loudly. "Fuck, you feel so good." I said, right before releasing deep inside her. I felt closer to her than ever and told her how much I love her and her body.

A few days later I stopped by the flower shop and when Tray informed me that Alicia had just been there.

"Really?" I didn't know what to think about that. "To give back your writing?"

"No, she already emailed me about my writing and I sent her the next chapter. She was just passing by and came in to say hello. I really like her, Ray, she's surprisingly cool."

"Yeah? What, you didn't think I would have a cool girlfriend?"

Tracy laughed a little defensively, "Oh no, I didn't mean that. I just think she looks really conservative, like a cheerleader almost, but then she says things that surprise me."

"Like?"

"Wouldn't you like to know?" Tracy smiled coyly, but then she went on. "Well, like I said, she looks like bubbly sunshine, but once I started talking to her I realized she definitely has some edge to her. She made a few funny and insightful comments about my book. Oh, and she is crazy about you, but you must know that." Tracy laughed.

"Yeah," I laughed, reminded of the blessing that I don't blush. "Pretty lucky for me."

"You are both lucky."

I was feeling a little self-conscious and I was ready to change the subject. "I brought your next chapter back and thought I would pick up some flowers for her while I am here."

"Oh yeah? Ready for red roses now?" She teased me.

"Oh, we're way past that. I'm ready for the 'I'd-love-you-even-if-your-butt-gets-big color'."

"Oh my god," Tracy laughed. "You are so funny. Hey, I know Alicia likes those hydrangeas over there."

"Really? Looks like something my Grandma would have in her yard. Pretty though."

"Yeah, they are really pretty. The colors within the flower are determined by the acid in the soil. You can put baking soda on the ground and they will turn into more of a pink."

"Whoa, that's cool. I like them blue like that."

"Well, so does Alicia," she confirmed as she walked over and started making up a bouquet. "And these are on the house."

227

"What? Tracy, I don't want to do that," I said, reaching for my wallet.

"I want to, Ray. I don't really make money off of guys like you anyway," she laughed. "Weddings are my bread and butter. Besides, you introduced me to two really cool people and I want to do something for you."

"Two? William?" I asked.

"Yeah, he's been emailing me too," she smiled. We talked about her writing for a while and she said William had pretty much the same opinion as I did but just used different adjectives. I laughed at that. "Maybe a double date is in our future?" I asked.

She smiled and said she wasn't sure William was attracted to her. "It might just be that he is interested in my writing. I'm not everyone's cup of tea, you know." She winked at me and gestured to her tattooed arm.

"Oh, you definitely have his number," I told her. As we said goodbye, I thought I'd better talk to William about not screwing around with my friend. I hated to think about Tracy just being his latest conquest.

A few days later Alicia asked me to come to a group counseling session with her at her outpatient program. Margaret would facilitate, and all the women in her recovery group would be bringing a family member or support person, so of course I would go. Having never been to such a thing, I really did not know what to expect. There were about twenty people there, all sitting in a circle on metal folding chairs. Margaret had us all introduce ourselves and state our relationship with the patient. There were boyfriends, husbands, moms, friends, and even a sibling there to support the women Alicia met with every day.

I recognized some of the women by name and remembered some of the things Alicia had told me about them, such as Melanie, who Alicia said was her favorite, someone she could hang out with. Then there was Sandra, who Alicia didn't think was ready to change. Ellen was one who always argued with Margaret, and Kim had serious anger issues. Sara was a bit older and one of the two married women. I noticed her husband, Doug, had body language of someone who is highly irritated. And then there was little Lily looking frail and scared.

Margaret spoke to the group about how things might change once the women finished the program and what kind of support they would need. She asked the group what their concerns were about after-care and Melanie's mom went first and got pretty emotional about the lying that went on and not feeling like she could believe anything her daughter said.

Ellen's fiancé spoke next and said he was concerned about ongoing health problems and Ellen's ability to be a healthy mother. He wanted a family and Ellen said she did too.

Lily's mom clasped her hand the whole time. She said a few words, but Lily just sat there and cowered. I felt really sorry for her. But not as sorry as I soon felt for Sara.

Doug actually said that Sara better not get fat. I heard a collective intake of breath and the room got quiet as I watched Sara fidget in her seat. I was surprised Margaret didn't say anything, so I interjected, "You mean really fat, right? Like obese, right?"

Doug looked at me and said to the group, "She was thin when we got married. I want her to stay that way. What's wrong with that?"

I stared at him and then looked at Sara who was looking down and not meeting anyone's eyes. He started to go on and on about how she had gotten chunky in the past and he had put up with so much from her. Why couldn't she be like other women and just control herself without going off the deep end? He used the word "fat" again and I felt myself getting increasingly annoyed. Doug wasn't anything special; Sara was definitely the better looking partner in the pair, yet he was so arrogant about how at work events and such he needed Sara to present herself well and he uttered the word "fat" again. I noticed Sara cringe every time and I was getting really upset. I started thinking, to myself, "Say fat one more time, asshole, and I am going to rip your head off," but he kept talking about what he expected from a wife and I glared at him, almost daring him to say fat once more so I could smash my fist into his face, but he didn't. Instead he babbled on about how yes of course he loved her, but he wasn't going to be phony and he didn't marry her expecting her to get fat and that is when rage got the better of me. The words came out of my mouth in a voice I did not recognize: "Say fat one more time, mother-fucker, say fat once more."

The room was silent with everyone staring at us and he looked at me in shock that quickly turned to anger and he drew the word out very slowly, "Fat."

I jumped out of my chair and charged towards him as he sprung out of his chair too. I got the first swing in, and he tried to duck, but it connected with the side of his head and he lost his footing and fell back towards the chairs and knocked it over causing it to hit the ground with a loud clang. But he regained his footing quickly and came back at me swinging. I saw his fist coming and ducked to miss his right hook and instinctively sunk a swift jab to his gut. It felt like time was going in slow motion, although in actuality it happened extremely fast and I was just reacting, but before I could land another punch, someone was holding my arm. Damn, two good hits and someone already intervened when I had him just where I wanted him.

I found out later there were a few guys holding me back

and there was a lot of chaos, a cacophony of yelling and crying going on but to me it all seemed a blur. Guys were pulling me, and Margaret was yelling at them to get me outside, but I just looked for Alicia's face to make sure she was okay. Her eyes were big but she was grinning.

Three guys pulled me outside and as soon as we got out the door, one of them went back inside while another said, "Thank goodness someone had the balls to do that," and he shook my hand, which seemed really odd. I was wondering why he hadn't done anything himself if he thought it was such a noble thing to do.

Alicia came running out the door and said, "Oh my God, Ray! I have never seen that side of you!" She was smiling, but then got a worried look on her face and said, "We'd better go. That ass is talking about calling the cops and pressing charges!"

"I'll stick up for you, man," the other guy said. "The fact that he stood up could be interpreted as provoking you and you defending yourself. That's what I would say as a witness, self-defense." He turned to Alicia and said, "He didn't get hurt too bad, did he?"

"Well, no, he isn't even bleeding, but his ego is damaged, badly damaged."

So Alicia and I scurried through the crowd on the sidewalk and made it to the station just as a train pulled up. We were laughing about our "getaway", but really I wasn't worried about being apprehended by the police. I might be a little worried if the guy was seriously hurt, but he wasn't.

When we got to Alicia's apartment, it took a while for my adrenaline to settle down, but after an hour I almost forgot about what happened except for the slight throbbing in my hand.

Then Margaret called. After talking to Alicia, she asked to speak to me. She said she was able to calm Doug down so he didn't call the police or file charges. I said thanks and that I owed her one, to which she answered, "Yes, you do, Ray. You owe me some therapy."

"What?" I exclaimed, feeling tricked. "I don't need therapy! That guy was a complete ass and I just did what everyone else was thinking."

"That may be true, Ray, but you pounced on him. I was watching you and while I think your anger was legitimate, it was a little out of skew for what was going on. I think you have some anger inside you that needs to be dealt with."

"What do you mean? I am a mellow guy– just ask Alicia."

"Well, Ray, it couldn't hurt and it might help. Besides, you owe me. Three sessions is all I ask."

And that is how I found myself in therapy, something I never would have planned. I came to learn that I had never properly grieved the loss of my mom, how I needed to forgive my dad, and how I had to find a way to express anger instead of keeping it inside and unloading with violence. Margaret had me take a look at some corny books about the stages of grief and one about loving someone who self-harms.

Margaret asked for three sessions but I ended up going for five extra and it wasn't bad at all. I think some of the things I learned will help me with Alicia and even with my dad, so all in all I am glad for Doug and his big fat mouth.

Alicia completed her outpatient program and started working full-time at her job. She found a good roommate situation with this guy named Victor. He seems pretty cool and very gay, but the best part was that he travels for work a lot so we will get the place to ourselves sometimes. Alicia really likes him and the apartment is stylish and clean. Apartments are so small in New York that it really helps if the roommate isn't into clutter or messy and Victor knows how to decorate.

I helped her pack up her old place and move. As we were putting her stuff away in the kitchen, Alicia showed me the inside of his refrigerator. "Look! I think Victor has man-o-rexia," she whispered. She vowed to be a healthy example to him as she proudly unpacked her oatmeal. "Carbs are your friend, Victor. Make peace with carbs," she whispered, although he wasn't even home.

We started running together and it was really fun at first, but then she started getting obsessed and, honestly, a bit too skinny —although I never said anything about that. It was mostly how intense she was getting about mileage and improving her time and it started becoming a drag. Luckily Margaret convinced her she was slipping into very dangerous territory right before Alicia signed up for a marathon. Alicia actually agreed to back off.

Alicia calls her parents every few days and works hard at mending that relationship. I am both relieved and surprised that they don't seem to hold any grudge against me. They even invited me to come to California for Christmas, so that is what we are planning to do. I'll get to meet Alicia's sisters and see where she grew up. Janice has called me a few times and tries to act like she is just being social, but then she always finds a way to ask, "So, how Alicia is *really* doing?" I can honestly answer that Alicia is doing really well.

I didn't tell her mom that we had our first fight because her work had a party with a bunch of food and Alicia got really anxious about it, thinking everyone was watching what she was eating or not eating. I was stoked to be around all that delicious free food and told Alicia she was being self-absorbed and everyone else was just thinking about themselves. She got angry and so did I. Then I realized that she gets nervous around social events associated with food, and I had better cut her some slack. On the flipside, she said I get giddy around free food – and I really can't deny that.

Then Alicia got something in the mail from her school, asking if she was going to register for the next semester. It wouldn't be until after Christmas, but I still felt my heart get heavy. I knew I would have to support her decision whichever way it went, but I loved being able to spend time with her.

I stayed quiet about it as I watched her mood get darker and darker. I know she talked to Margaret about the school situation, but I stayed out of it and waited to hear whatever choice she made. Then one night, while we were lying side-by-side in bed she turned to me and asked, "Ray, will you still love me if I don't become a CPA?"

"What?!" I laughed, but she was looking at me all insecure and I could see she was actually serious. "Alicia, I couldn't care less about that."

"But when you met me I was a go-getter. You won't be disappointed or think of me as a slacker?"

I paused rather than answer right away. This sounded ridiculous, but I could see that it was a really serious issue for her, so I took a deep breath before answering. "I wasn't looking for a CPA. I wasn't looking for anything, really. But then you came along and changed my life. I didn't fall in love with you because you are ambitious. I fell in love with you because you are sweet and brave and shy and beautiful. I love how you are curious and enthusiastic about stuff, how you look things up. I like how you get so excited about New York, you're like a little kid, and your enthusiasm is contagious. I love how friendly and outgoing you are to everyone you meet. You make a really good impression on people; you are warm and they like you. Plus, you are really smart, and did I mention beautiful? And sexy as hell too. And I love you because you love me. At a low point in my life, you could still see that I was a good person, a worthy person, when I could no longer see it myself. I couldn't care less if you become a CPA. The main thing I want is for you to be happy and healthy, whatever that takes. I want you to be with me for life. For a long life. I'm completely in love with you."

Alicia had a tear on her cheek, so I wiped it away, finally a happy tear I could kiss away. And kiss away I did.

Epilogue:

It's almost summer here again in New York. The Klaer family is planning a big backpacking trip out in California and they want Alicia and me to come out and join them. Steve keeps asking Alicia about my experience with the great outdoors and specifically if I have ever slept outside. Alicia and I have laughed about that a lot. Yeah, I've slept outdoors in all kinds of weather. Sleeping in a tent with a sleeping bag sounds like five-star accommodations to me, so Alicia assured Steve I would be fine. I'm really looking forward to it, plus it will give me a chance to talk to Steve about something important. I have my mom's ring and I thought about asking Alicia to marry me in some beautiful setting like Yosemite. Or maybe on top of a mountain, or next to a stream or waterfall. Then I realized that I would rather wait until we get back and propose in Central Park. I want to ask Alicia to marry me in New York City. We are New Yorkers, after all, and this seems right. New York is our home.

Afterword:

This is a story about love and redemption. In the beginning, it seems that Ray is the one with the problems, but the reader learns that Alicia is the one in real trouble. Part way through this writing, I was blessed with the help of an amazing editor, "Lovely Bob," who appreciated and understood what I was trying to convey. During our back-and-forth communications, he asked some background questions and, given the serious topic of the eating disorder bulimia nervosa, he felt it was worthwhile to share some of our conversation with the reader. Here is part of what we discussed behind the scenes:

Q. *Donna, are you yourself bulimic?*

A. No. I definitely have other issues and have been in recovery for a very long time, but I have always had a very healthy relationship with food.

Q. *Are you a therapist? Do you have advanced training in the treatment of eating disorders?*

A. No, not at all. After overcoming my own difficulties, I went to school to become a Health teacher. I wanted to teach teenagers about the dangers of drug and alcohol abuse, about eating disorders, sex education, including STDs - you know, all the interesting topics! But I fell in love with Biology during my schooling and became a Bio teacher instead.

Q. *What elements of these real-world experiences made their way into the story of Alicia and Ray?*

A. Tons. Too many to list. As far as Ray goes, I know what it is like to be down and out. I know what it is like to crawl out of a hole. And Alicia? Even though I have never had an eating disorder myself, I have been a mentor for several women who do. The scratched hands, the use of markers, the heart attack, the unrealistic body expectations, the over-exercising, even the puking in jars all came from real people in my life. And so did the outpatient program and the "Texas Toast" too.

Q. *In your opinion, what does it take to "beat" bulimia?*

A. Well, as we have discussed, I am no expert! I am a writer and this is a fictional story with a positive ending, but it easily could have gone the other way. I knew it could not be a girl-meets-boy-and-instantly-gets-better story. I believe what William said, "You can't fix this, Ray," and what Steve Klaer said, "Love doesn't fix this." But love helps! And the most important love when it comes to recovery from bulimia, is the love that comes from inside. When I started this story, I thought that Alicia would not recover and would break Ray's heart, but she proved to be more of a fighter than I had planned. I asked myself, "What would it take for Alicia to recover?" And what I came up with is the following things that I knew had to happen in the story:

1. A critical event. This is the proverbial wake-up call. In Alicia's case it was her heart attack. All by itself this event would most likely not be enough to cause a change. People endure horrible things and continue destructive behavior, but it did bring Alicia's trouble out into the open.

2. A genuine, inner desire to change. Wanting to please your lover or your parents isn't enough. The desire must be grounded in a concern for your own welfare. A genuine love of self is paramount.

3. Divine intervention. The feisty old lady Ray encountered in church ("God sees everything, and I see plenty.") is praying for Alicia (and for Ray, too).

4. Professional help, both medical and psychological. Alicia has found a good therapist in Margaret, and an outpatient treatment program that works for her.

5. Support. Steve and Janice Klaer are frustrated with Alicia but they still love her. Ray loves her and is committed to making a life with her. But they can't understand what suffering with bulimia means. The friends Alicia is making in Margaret's outpatient therapy group are her co-sufferers and are an important part of her recovery.

6. Confronting and dealing with underlying issues. Alicia somehow got herself stuck with the attitude that she had to be perfect in order to earn love. Overcoming her perfectionism is part of her recovery from bulimia.

7. Replacing unhealthy behaviors with new healthy habits. Alicia takes up running. Unfortunately, she starts getting obsessive about the new behavior, but that problem is dealt with in counseling.

8. Acceptance of body issues. In this final chapter, Ray has tried to help Alicia recognize the beauty and sexual appeal of a variety of body shapes and sizes.

9. The ability to laugh at oneself. Alicia admitting that she puked in jars and laughing about how gross it was is one example, but I think this is something she will grow into over time. Her most playful side has been demonstrated in her sexuality. And there's no denying: Alicia has a very healthy libido!

Q. *Do you identify with Alicia?*

A. I actually identify much more with Ray than with Alicia.

Q.: *What do you admire most about Ray?*

A. Ray's experience at being nearly homeless matured him and he is very tolerant. I like how he evolved throughout the story. He went from being anti-social to being comfortable around a variety of people. A librarian, Alicia's parents, the therapist, soccer players, neighbors, and a homeless guy were among his friends. I appreciate that he was a reader and a learner, although not formally educated. He started out thinking he was invisible and not worthy of anybody's attention, but by the end of the story he had job skills, friends, and love. He even felt like he had something to give back. Ray climbed Maslow's pyramid. And he finally felt at home in the big city.

RAY KELLY'S RECOMMENDED READING LIST

Extremely Loud and Incredibly Close, by Jonathan Safran Foer

Let the Great World Spin, by Colum McCann

The Amazing Adventures of Kavalier & Clay, by Michael Chabon

The Catcher In the Rye, by JD Salinger

The Memory of Running, by Ron McLarty

The Buffalo Hunter, by Peter Straub

The Power of the Dog, by Thomas Savage

I would like to extend a sincere
and heartfelt thanks to
Aaron, Erin, Jill, Michelle, Rebecca, and Yoshi.

More information about the author, visit:

DonnaBeckWrites.com

Next in the series:

Flower Girl – coming Spring of 2015

18662011R00144

Made in the USA
San Bernardino, CA
23 January 2015